A ROGUE MEETS A SCANDALOUS LADY

MACKENZIES SERIES, BOOK 11

JENNIFER ASHLEY

JA / AG PUBLISHING

CHAPTER 1

February, 1893

When the pistol flashed down Regent's Park's green, David Fleming realized his life truly needed to change.

He danced aside as the bullet whined past him, but his unsteady body took him down to the earth, coating his pristine black cashmere suit in mud and grass. David tasted dirt as gravel cut his cheek.

"What the devil are you doing?" Pickering, his second, shouted down at him. "Get up, man. Return the shot."

David groaned as he rolled over, his finger well away from the trigger of his revolver. He felt little pain, because the whisky he'd drunk all night, neat, erased almost all sensation.

"Anyone hit?" he slurred.

Pickering glanced around at the small crowd of gentlemen gathered in the dawn light, his fair hair twitching in the breeze. "Don't think so."

David tried to get his legs under him, couldn't, and stuck up his arm to Pickering. "Help me."

It took Pickering a few moments to realize David was talking to him. Idiot. Finally Pickering hauled David to his feet. Their cronies, young and old, waited without much concern.

"You forfeit," said an older gentleman with side-whiskers, who should have known better than to be in Regent's Park at the crack of dawn, encouraging duels. "Griffin wins."

David scrubbed at the mud on his silk waistcoat. "What the hell are we doing, gentlemen? A *duel*? In this day and age? You were expecting to watch us kill each other."

"An honorable way to settle differences," the older gentleman said calmly.

He was interrupted by a roar as David's opponent, a hothead called Oliver Griffin, rushed at him.

"Coward!" Griffin bellowed. "Cheat! Stand still and let me shoot you."

He waved his pistol in a shaky hand, which Pickering, in alarm, yanked from his grasp. Griffin swayed mightily, as drunk as the rest of them, but he managed to lock his hands around David's neck.

"Settle it like gentlemen, you said," he seethed, his spittle showering David. "I'll settle *you*—"

Griffin held on like a leech. David scrabbled at Griffin's impossibly tight grip then decided it was time to forget about being a gentleman.

He brought up his fist in a perfect pugilist move to crack Griffin's chin. If David jerked that chin to the side he could snap Griffin's neck, but he had no intention of being hauled in for murder this morning. He pushed Griffin off balance then followed up with a smart punch to the man's eye.

Griffin howled. David slid from him and steadied himself on his feet, using Pickering's shoulder for support.

"It is done," he proclaimed to Griffin in a voice men had learned to obey. "We met, you shot. Honor is satisfied. Rules of the game."

Griffin turned, his face bloody. "You have no honor, Fleming. I'll kill you! How do I know my sons are even mine? Cuckoos in my nest ..."

David slid his handkerchief from his pocket and dabbed at the cuts on his cheek. Futile, because the handkerchief was just as grimy as his face.

"I never touched your wife, Griff. She's an honorable lady and loyal to you, Lord knows why. Be kind to her."

Griffin only snarled. He'd been so convinced that his wife was having an *affaire de coeur* with the notorious David Fleming that he hadn't stopped to ascertain whether it was true. Griffin's wife was the friend of the Duchess of Kilmorgan, and when the duchess had instructed David to look after Mrs. Griffin at a ball a week ago, David leapt to obey.

If he flirted with the woman, he wasn't to be blamed. She was lonely, unhappy, and married to the boorish Griffin. She'd enjoyed being the center of attention for a few hours, but neither of them had had any intention of taking it further.

Griffin closed his mouth but a look of cunning came over his face. "I don't believe you, but it doesn't matter. I've had my revenge. Ask your darling countess where *she's* been this past week." Instead of leaving it cryptic, Griffin jabbed at his own chest. "With *me*. I've had her, Fleming. In every way possible." He thrust out his pelvis and his friends laughed.

"Poor woman," David said feelingly. He carefully folded his muddy handkerchief and tucked it into his breast pocket. If Griffin wanted his vengeance using David's current mistress, a countess from Bavaria, he was welcome to it. She was an amorous lady, not bothered by which bed she slept in of nights. "No wonder she's been looking peaky. Do give her my best when you see her again."

Time to tip his hat and walk away. Except David couldn't find his hat. Blast it all, he hated to lose it—it was a fine piece of headgear.

He heard another bellow, and damned if Griffin wasn't coming at him again.

How the devil had he let himself be talked into this duel, of all things?

He'd been drunk, that was how. Drunk, weary, and bored, and decided shooting at Griffin would be good fun. But now he was aching and wanted to go home.

David sidestepped as Griffin lunged at him, got the man in a headlock and tidily flipped him onto his back. He'd learned that move from Hart Mackenzie—after Hart had done it to him.

Griffin cursed and howled. Griffin's friends, cretins, the lot of them, decided David was being unfair, and as one, they threw themselves at him. David went down in a scrum, blows landing on his face, back, arms, his ribs creaking as boots connected with his side.

Above the shouting and swearing came the shrill, piercing whistles of Peelers with arrests on their minds.

The men jerked upright and then dispersed, bolting into the mists. Even Pickering and the older gentleman deserted David, leaving him to the mad rush of dark-suited, helmeted men who pounded toward him.

A muscular arm hauled David to his feet. "You're under arrest, sir," the bobby told him cheerfully. "Causing a disturbance and discharging a firearm."

"If you'll note, constable, *my* firearm wasn't discharged,"

David began, but the words slurred into nothing as the constable closed a metal cuff around his wrist.

———————

As JAILS WENT, IT WAS NOT TOO BAD, DAVID DECIDED. THE lockup on Marylebone Road consisted of one small room where the arrests of the night waited for the magistrate's decisions in the morning. David had commandeered a place by the wall, bribing the inhabitants to not steal every piece of clothing on his body by parting with all the coins in his purse. His watch would be next. A man with only one eye kept that eye on it.

The place stank and was filthy, the bodies of sleeping men heaped on the floor. Vermin scratched in dark corners. But at least there was a window, high above, that let them know the sun had fully risen.

Any request that word be taken to David's solicitor, his valet, his very good friend the Duke of Kilmorgan—or even a random person in the street—had been ignored. The constables who'd dragged him from the park had pushed David in with the other arrests of the night and left him. Now here he lay.

Did the bottom of the slope feel like this?

David's head pounded, his throat was on fire, and his stomach roiled. All he wanted was more whisky to soothe the pain. That and a soft bed, a beautiful woman, and perhaps a cigar.

No, the thought of smoke brought on more nausea. He'd leave the cigar until he felt better.

The door creaked. "Mr. Fleming!" The turnkey bellowed the name without interest.

David climbed painfully to his feet. "Here I am, my good fellow. Have you brought my breakfast?"

A few of the inmates guffawed. "Aye, fetch me a mess of bangers and a bucket of coffee," one croaked.

The turnkey ignored them, his balefulness all for David. "Come on, you."

A bit early to see the magistrate, David mused, though perhaps the man wanted to make a start on his cases for the day. Thieves of apples, handkerchiefs, and children's clothes; ladies selling favors; and David.

He followed the turnkey through a dank passage to a larger room that was empty but for a table and chair. A burly constable joined them and pushed David into the seat.

"Thank you, sir," David said to the turnkey. "Kind of you to show me to my parlor."

"Shut it," the constable said as the turnkey growled and left them. "When the Super comes, you be respectful."

"Superintendent, is he?" David said. "My, I am moving in high circles now."

The constable hit him. A blow across the mouth, not hard enough to draw blood, but enough to make David's head rock back. "I *said*, shut it."

David heaved an aggrieved sigh. He held up his hands as the constable bunched his fist again, and made the motion of turning a key over his lips.

The door opened once more to admit a tall man. David's first instinct was to rise, because the gentleman who entered was one of distinction, but the constable's warning glare kept him to his seat.

Hazel eyes in a hard face met David's, hair that was just touched with red glinted in the bad light. He had the height, the build, and the manner of Hart Mackenzie, the Duke of Kilmorgan, but he wasn't Hart. It was his half-brother, Detective Superintendent Lloyd Fellows.

David relaxed in relief until he saw the frost in Fellows's gaze.

"Oh, come now," David said, giving him his most charming smile. "You don't truly believe I was trying to shoot a man in Regent's Park, no matter how much he goaded me. If you examine my pistol, you'll find it fully loaded and un-fired."

Fellows's face remained granite hard. "Griffin has brought charges of assault and attempted murder on you, and his earl uncle is calling for your blood."

"For pity's sake." David pointed to the bruises on his face. He was plastered with mud, still a bit drunk, and spattered with dried blood. "Does *this* look like I assaulted myself? A solicitor would be a fine thing, Detective Super."

"I have recommended that the magistrate let you return home until this is sorted. He does not like the idea, but he bows to the might of the Duke of Kilmorgan."

David heaved a sigh of gratitude. God himself would bow to the might of Hart Mackenzie.

He rose. "Good old Hart. Thank you, Fellows."

"Sit down." Fellows pointed at the hard chair. David obediently sat, wincing from his bruises.

"It's a serious accusation, Fleming. One that could get you hanged, or at the very least, sent to Dartmoor. Doesn't matter who your connections are—you're not a peer, so you'll be tried at the Old Bailey with everyone else."

"Griff has to prove it," David said. "I do know that much about the laws of jolly England. Innocent until a jury says I'm guilty." He spread his hands on the unclean table. "I did not discharge my pistol, I promise you. I ducked when Griffin discharged *his* at *me*. I don't know why I bothered—he's a rotten shot."

"I convinced the magistrate there was no immediate evidence

to suggest you tried to kill Mr. Griffin. However, many witnessed the ensuing fight. You can bring counter charges against him, of course."

"Bugger that." David once again surged to his feet. "If I'm not being charged, I believe I am free to leave."

Fellows gave him a nod, but a grim one. "Don't flee to the Continent. I have a friend in the Sûreté, and he'd find you, but you'd rather he didn't. I hear you have an estate in Hertfordshire. Perhaps lying low there for a time is a good idea."

David shuddered. His ancestral home—Moreland Park—held too many foul memories. "I will retreat to my London house, pour coffee down my throat, soak in a bath, and sleep for a week. With that satisfy the magistrate?"

"I doubt it." The dry tone in Fellows's voice was something he shared with Hart—that edge that told its recipient he was a damned fool. "Before you withdraw from the world, the duchess requests that you call upon her."

David sank to the chair again, his strength gone. "She does, does she?"

Fellows, David could spar with. Hart Mackenzie, he could face. Hart's wife, Eleanor ... that was another matter entirely.

"Please tell her I am suddenly stricken with a dire disease and must quarantine myself in my house with a cask of whisky."

Fellows regarded him in some pity. "Tell her yourself." He tapped the table once, turned, and walked out.

"Heaven help me," David muttered. It was some time before he made himself rise and follow the impatient constable out.

———

DAVID KEPT A STASH OF MACKENZIE MALT IN HIS CARRIAGE

for emergencies. He imbibed a little now to clear his head as his coachman took him to Grosvenor Square.

The Duke of Kilmorgan owned a tall house on one side of the square, which dominated all others around it. The house had been in the family since the late eighteenth century, when the Mackenzie family had begun to prosper once more. The Battle of Culloden, in which they'd fought on the side of the Jacobites, had nearly wiped them out. But the canny Mackenzies had managed to regain their title taken from them as traitors to the crown and recover their fortune. They'd bought the house that had been owned by the Marquess of Ellesmere, and swarmed in.

David was distantly related to the family through his ancestor aunt who had married Angus Mackenzie, the son of the glorious Malcolm Mackenzie and his English wife, Mary.

The distance was everything, David thought as he stared up at the house. Hart was a duke, and his brothers had courtesy titles, large houses, and plenty of money. David, the shirttail relative, was still in his evening dress from the night before, thoroughly coated with mud, and coming tamely to the house when sent for.

Eleanor would be waiting in her parlor, rustling in some silken gown Hart would have bought her. Her red hair would glisten, and she'd have a secret smile on her face that betrayed she was a woman in love—with Hart, of course. There had never been anyone else for Eleanor.

She'd gaze at David with her cornflower blue eyes and ask bluntly what sort of scrape he'd gotten himself into now.

David wouldn't mind, except that once upon a time, he'd been madly in love with the dratted woman. He'd asked her to marry him, and she'd turned him down with a speed that had made his head spin.

He still cared for her, but the burning passion had subsided.

Eleanor and Hart belonged together, and no one could tear them asunder. So be it.

David took another gulp of whisky, which burned to his empty stomach.

He held up the flask in salute. "Apologies, dear El, but you are the one thing I cannot face today." He rapped his stick on the roof. "Hinch!"

A tiny trap door opened, and the eye of his large coachman blinked at him. "Yes, guv?"

"Change of plans. Take me ..." Home? No. His valet, Fortescue, would fuss, and his housekeeper would try to bring him soup, like an invalid. Someone would send word to Hart, and Eleanor would corner him. Or his solicitor would pop by to discuss the grave charges, or Griffin would send his solicitors to threaten David.

London wouldn't do, and neither would Hertfordshire. Scotland? No, too many Mackenzies in Scotland.

There was only one place in the world David could think to go, and he wasn't certain of his welcome even there.

"To Shropshire," he finished.

Hinch's eye widened. "Guv? Ye want me to drive you all the way to Shropshire?"

"Yes. If we make a start, we'll arrive early tomorrow morning."

"But it's me wife's birthday." The red-rimmed eye held pleading.

David heaved a sigh. "You're right, Hinchie. I'm being selfish. Take me to a station and get me on a train heading west. Then do as you please."

"Thank ye, guv." Hinch vanished. The carriage jerked forward, nearly dislodging David from the seat, and made at a swift pace for Euston Station.

DAVID HAD LITTLE RECOLLECTION OF THE JOURNEY. HE swayed in the first class carriage alone, finishing off his flask before a waiter helpfully brought him champagne. He had little to eat, as he doubted his ability to keep anything down.

The Shropshire hamlet he aimed for lay well south of Shrewsbury. David had to change trains several times, assisted onto the last, small chugging train by a stationmaster who more or less hoisted him aboard and dropped him into a seat.

By the time they reached the village three miles from David's destination, he was well inebriated and mostly asleep. He vaguely remembered being escorted from the train and pushed onto a dogcart as he mumbled the direction.

The jolting, sickening cart finally halted then listed as the driver climbed down. "You're here, guv."

Here was very, very dark, and utterly cold. David had no recollection of what he was doing or where he'd been trying to reach.

Light shone in his face, and David cringed. The driver and another man who'd joined them hauled David out of the cart and to his feet, but David promptly collapsed as soon as they let him go.

He fell on wet paving stones with grass between them. The boots in front of him drew back, and a face bent toward him. The head was shaggy and a white noose encircled its neck. David flung up his hands, crying out.

"Good heavens," a rumbling voice said, and the face resolved into one of comforting familiarity. The white noose, David realized, was the collar of a country vicar.

"Sanctuary," David whispered.

The vicar stared at David for a time before he let out a sigh. "Help me get him inside," he said to the driver.

The next memory David had after that was light.

Far too much light, pounding through his eyelids and searing at his temples. He groaned.

The sound was loud, and David cut it off. He lay for a long time in dire misery before he realized he was in a bed piled high with quilts, a rather comfortable one at that.

The bedroom was tiny, with whitewashed walls, the ceiling sloping abruptly down to the eaves. David discovered this fact when he sat up and banged his head on a roof beam. A window about four feet square let in the dazzling sunlight.

His coat and waistcoat had been removed, but not his trousers. He tried very hard to remember where he was and why he'd come here, but at the moment, all was a blur.

When he at last dragged himself from the bed, David couldn't find his coat, but a dressing gown had been draped over a chair. Ah, well, the inhabitants of this house would have to take David as he came.

David struggled with the dressing gown, only managing to get one arm inside before he found the door to the bedroom and opened it. This led onto a landing, no other doors around it. If he hadn't hesitated on the threshold, he'd have plunged straight down the stairs.

Recollection about where he was grew as he went down the staircase, its wood dark with time. At the bottom lay a whitewashed passage that ran the length of the cottage. If David remembered aright, *this* door led to a dining room. He didn't particularly want food, but Dr. Pierson would have thick, strong coffee, and at the moment, it was all David craved.

He chose the correct door, stumbled into the room, and collapsed onto a chair on one side of the table, eyes closing. He slumped forward, forehead resting on the polished table, and let out another groan.

A hot beverage slid toward him. David could tell by the scent that curled into his nose that it was tea.

"Coffee," he mumbled. "For the love of God."

"Tea might be a wee bit better in your condition," a light voice said. "I've read books on the matter."

The speaker was not Dr. Pierson, David's longtime friend and sometime mentor, a burly man with a beard and a rumbling voice. This voice held a clarity that slid through David's stupor and touched something deep inside him.

He raised his head—carefully.

And beheld the most beautiful woman in the world. She sat across the table from him, surrounded by a halo of light, and gazed at him with unblinking green eyes.

CHAPTER 2

*I*s he quite all right?" Sophie asked her uncle.

Lucas Pierson, the vicar of this parish, shook his head and raised a cup of tea to his bearded lips. "Not really."

Sophie studied the lump of humanity who'd landed at Uncle Lucas's breakfast table. He'd managed to get one arm into Uncle's best dressing gown but no more. The other arm lay on the table in a soiled shirt sleeve, the cuff open to reveal a sinewy hand and part of a well-muscled forearm.

A tangled mess of dark brown hair covered the head partly raised, as did dirt and bits of grass. His face was brushed with a shadow that said he'd missed a shave for two or three days. The rest of the face was interesting—square shape, nose not too long but not small, skin rather pale, the lightness of the far north, Scotland perhaps.

His eyes, though. Sophie's teacup hesitated on the way to her lips. She was not certain of the color just now—blue, she thought, or gray, or some shade in between. A lake on a cloudy day.

Those eyes were intense and, even though now bloodshot,

held strength of will that kept Sophie from glancing away from him.

"Does he speak at all?" Sophie asked.

Uncle Lucas chuckled. "Sometimes far too much. My dear, this sorry specimen is my old friend, Mr. David Fleming. I look upon him as a reprobate son or younger brother, as my mood takes me." He raised his voice and directed his next words to the motionless, staring form. "David, if you can understand me, this is my niece, Sophie ... er, Tierney."

Sophie tried not to flinch at Uncle's hesitation, and held her breath, waiting for Mr. Fleming's reaction. Uncle Lucas hadn't used Sophie's married name, but as everything about her had been dragged through the newspapers sideways, Mr. Fleming must certainly have read her history.

The gray-blue eyes blinked a few times, no recognition in them. "Pleased to meet you, Miss Tierney." The deep voice grated somewhat, as though he'd not drunk water in a fortnight. "Forgive my present, deplorable state. I ..." He slumped to the tabletop. "It is a long story."

Sophie let out her breath in relief. Mr. Fleming hadn't heard of her, or at least did not remember in his wretched condition. Odd, but she'd be grateful for it. She'd sought sanctuary here, in Uncle Lucas's out-of-the-way parish in a corner of Shropshire. Here she could be merely Dr. Pierson's niece, not the notorious Lady Devonport, the Whore of Babylon.

She studied the man across from her with more interest. Sophie had heard of her uncle's friend, Mr. Fleming, but she'd never met him. He was a colleague of the Duke of Kilmorgan, a scandalous Scotsman who dressed in kilts and vowed to make Scotland an independent nation.

Sophie's husband, Laurie Whitfield, the Earl of Devonport,

was in a decidedly anti-Scots faction, and she'd never been invited into the Duchess of Kilmorgan's circle.

Mr. Fleming had a breathtaking presence, even in this stage between inebriation and illness. His half-dressed state fascinated her—Sophie's husband remained completely clothed at all times, except when he became babe-naked for his half hour attempt to beget an heir on her.

Mr. Fleming would be a handsome gentleman if he cleaned up a bit, not that Sophie was interested in handsome gentlemen. They could stay far, far away, thank you very much.

She lifted her teacup, managing to take a sip this time. "Did you have a wrestling match with a lawn?" she asked him.

"Very amusing." Mr. Fleming's slurring voice was touched with Scots, but only a touch. "It was a close-run thing, but the lawn finally let me go."

Sophie chuckled. He was so self-deprecating that she couldn't help it. She'd had her fill of arrogant men who could do no wrong.

A fleeting smile touched his mouth, increasing his handsomeness. A dangerous man, Sophie concluded. No lady would be safe with him. She sipped tea and felt momentary envy for those ladies.

"I had no idea you had company, Pierson." Mr. Fleming attempted to lift his teacup, but his fingers shook so much, the tea slopped over. "I beg your pardon. I can take myself off." He sucked tea from his fingertips, mouth puckering in inadvertent sensuality.

"You're in no condition to take yourself anywhere," Uncle Lucas said sternly. "I imagine you were running from the law or an angry husband or furious MPs. Or all three. Stay until you're in fighting form again. I imagine that's why you sought me out."

Mr. Fleming winced at his blunt speech. "Delicate ears, Pierson."

"I keep no secrets from my niece. If I allow a man to stay under the same roof as she, she deserves to know the truth about him."

"I have no wish to cause a scandal." Mr. Fleming sat up straight in an attempt to draw his dignity around him. A lock of hair fell over one eye. When he tried to brush it back, the loose sleeve of the dressing gown caught on his saucer and sent it to the floor with a crash. "Damnation." He started to reach for the saucer, then grabbed his head and righted himself, falling back into the chair. "*Bloody* hell ... Sorry, Miss Tierney. I am a lout this morning."

Sophie was laughing again. "Drink the tea, sir. All of it. It's oolong. It will do you good."

"No wish to cause a scandal?" Uncle Lucas asked Mr. Fleming in surprise. Uncle took a hearty bite of his eggs and toast, which made Mr. Fleming go a bit green. "You mean one different from the others you've caused in your lifetime?"

"Miss Tierney is unchaperoned." Mr. Fleming's admonition, like a maiden aunt's, was so out of place that Sophie's amusement grew.

"I am her chaperone," Uncle Lucas said emphatically. "Besides, she's a married woman. Also seeking sanctuary."

"Why?" Mr. Fleming at last got the teacup to his mouth. He took a gulp of the contents and swallowed, the green tinge leaving his skin. "Is her husband a boor?"

He truly hadn't heard of her. Sophie sent her uncle a warning look before she rose from her chair. "If you'll excuse me one moment, I'll bring you something to soothe your ills, Mr. Fleming."

Mr. Fleming realized she was standing and hauled himself to his feet.

He was tall. Very tall. Laurie stood shorter than Sophie by a good inch, which always made her feel awkward and others titter. She made certain never to wear high-heeled slippers near him. Mr. Fleming would not make his lady feel awkward, and she could wear as high a heel as she wished.

At the moment, his height didn't agree with him. Mr. Fleming swayed mightily, and Sophie skimmed from the room so the poor man could sit down again.

She bustled to the kitchen and through it to the larder beyond. Mrs. Corcoran, the cook and housekeeper, gave Sophie a nod, asking if she could be of any help. The lady was used to Sophie running in and out to mix her herbal concoctions or ask for a recipe.

Sophie's happiest times in girlhood had been her visits to her uncle in Shropshire. Uncle Lucas, a lifelong bachelor, lived a simple life tending his parish, writing sermons, and researching Britain's deep past.

Sanctuary indeed. Here, the intervening years fell away—the giddiness of Sophie's debutante days, the strange excitement of her grand wedding, the disillusionment that married life brought. Next had come the disappointment when she didn't conceive, and finally anguish when Laurie decided to exchange her for a new wife.

The divorce case had yet to commence—the solicitors were putting arguments together for the long and complicated process. Laurie had decided to blame everything on Sophie and drag her through the mud.

Unable to take the betrayal in her own household, Sophie had fled to Uncle's vicarage, to the one place she could find peace. Even visiting her parents brought no relief, as they were sorrowful and upset about the whole turn of events. Uncle, upon her unexpected arrival, had merely said, "Ah there you are, my dear. Have a look at this map—a survey from the seventeenth century. It plots the old Roman settlements excellently."

Mr. Fleming appeared as though he'd been dragged through the mud, quite literally. As Sophie mixed her potion, making certain to put in plenty of cayenne, she realized that for the first time in a long while, Mr. Fleming had made her interested in another person. She'd been so sunk in her own defeat that even conversing on the weather had been a chore, and she'd avoided her friends—the ones still speaking to her, that is.

She shook the herbs, egg, and spices together, poured the concoction into a glass, and carried it out, thanking Mrs. Corcoran as she went.

"There." Sophie set the glass in front of Mr. Fleming as he struggled to rise upon her entrance. "No, please do not get up. I believe it would be quite dangerous for you."

Mr. Fleming sank from the half-standing position he'd managed and eyed the gray-green mixture in the glass with suspicion. "What the devil is *that*?"

"A cure for your condition. Or at least a palliative. You'll feel much better once it's down."

Sophie resumed her seat and finished her last piece of toast— loaded with butter, the way she liked it.

"I'd take her advice," Uncle Lucas said. "Her little potions do amazing things for me when I take cold."

Mr. Fleming tapped the glass. "It looks like sick. Smells like it too."

"Perhaps Uncle should hold your nose while I pour it into your mouth," Sophie said as she munched.

Mr. Fleming glared at her. "Did *you* raise your niece to be so cheeky, Pierson? Or does it run in the family?"

"Drink the potion," Uncle Lucas ordered. "As you are staying in my house, I would like you to be less bearlike and more amenable to bathing."

Mr. Fleming looked hurt. "I told you I'd take myself off."

"And I know you have nowhere to go, else you'd have gone there instead. You only seek me when you're at the end of your tether." Uncle gave him a severe look. "Drink."

Mr. Fleming eyed Sophie again. She took a noisy sip of tea, meeting his gaze squarely.

Mr. Fleming heaved a long sigh. He held his own nose and took a large swallow from the glass.

He had to let go of both nose and glass to cough. He fumbled for a handkerchief and didn't find one, so he coughed into the sleeve of Uncle's dressing gown. But the potion stayed down.

"What did you put into this?" he rasped at Sophie. "Oil of vitriol?"

"Only things growing in Uncle's garden. And from the market—wherever Mrs. Corcoran obtains her comestibles."

"Belladonna?" he snapped. "I imagine that grows in the garden." Mr. Fleming drew another long breath and took a second swallow. "Oil of vitriol, I swear it."

"Nonsense. It's a bit of pepper to warm your stomach."

"Warm it? Or set it on fire?" Mr. Fleming coughed again, but already he sounded stronger.

"My mother swears by it," Sophie said. "Helped my grandfather no end."

"I can bear witness to that," Uncle Lucas said.

"He lived a long and happy life, your grandfather?" Mr. Fleming growled.

"Indeed," Sophie said. "Passed away at a ripe old age, falling off his horse."

Mr. Fleming sent her a dark look. "Very encouraging." Sophie noticed that he finished the drink.

Uncle Lucas leaned his elbows on the table. "Get some breakfast down you, Fleming, then clean yourself up. Now that you're here, you can help work on my villa."

Mr. Fleming groaned. "You're not still hunting for *that*, are you? I thought you'd given up years ago."

"Of course I haven't given up," Uncle said in a tone bordering on shock. "It's there, mark my words."

Sophie sympathized with Mr. Fleming's dismay. Uncle had been scrambling around the knobby hills beyond the vicarage for years, convinced a Roman villa lay buried beneath the thick grass and scrub. He'd once found the remains of an ancient brooch of forged gold, and he was convinced that a wealthy Roman, or at least a Romanized Briton, had built a vast country estate somewhere nearby.

"A walk sounds lovely, Uncle."

Mr. Fleming only glowered, but reached for a piece of toast from the platter on the table, scattering crumbs as he ate.

"ONLY *YOU* WOULD DRAG A MAN IN MY CONDITION OUT INTO the freezing mist at the crack of dawn," David grumbled as he trudged the familiar path past the village church and out into the fields.

The sun was shining in spite of the earlier fog, and the day would be fine, if cold. David knew he should rejoice in the chance of fair weather, should skip and hop as though thrilled to be out of doors, and any moment sing along with the birdsong. He tramped forward, huddled in his coat, wondering why the bedamned birds had to sing so loudly.

He had to admit, however, that birds twittering in the trees, tiny lambs like puffs of wool on the green, and the clearing blue sky to show the ruined abbey on a far hill was a damn sight better than smoky London with dullards trying to shoot him, then banging him up for assault.

The company was much better too. Dr. Pierson was the sort of no-nonsense fellow David needed right now, and his niece ...

David realized Pierson had nattered on about his niece in the past, but he'd pictured a schoolgirl in braids and never thought a thing about her. David had even heard Pierson tell him she'd married, but again, he'd had the fleeting image of a simpering young bride and then forgot about her.

He hadn't been prepared for the black-haired beauty with green eyes and a straightforward stare who'd gazed at him fearlessly across the breakfast table. Still less prepared for her frank assessment of his half-inebriated, half-hungover state, which had obviously not impressed her.

David was used to women fawning over him no matter how he appeared. He did not confuse this fawning with delight or love or a natural reaction to the glory that was David Fleming. The ladies usually wanted something from him—money, favors, escape from their narrow lives for a few hours.

Sophie Tierney didn't need anything from David. He was her uncle's old friend, and that was all. She saw past his flummery and sardonic sneer to the very sad man behind it. And again, was not impressed.

She'd dressed sensibly for the outing, he noted. Female fashion had discarded the massive bustle, replacing it with sleeves so ballooning that David expected the ladies to be lifted off the ground at the first puff of wind. Miss Tierney, however, had eschewed the new style, at least for this country tramp. Her blouse was plain over a narrow skirt, and she wore a long jacket against the cold, and stout boots. No billowing sleeves in sight. Her wide-brimmed hat was large enough to keep off the sun and any rain that might fall.

David had left clothes at the vicarage over the years, which Mrs. Corcoran kept clean for him, so he had a suitable ensemble for slogging through muddy fields. It wasn't often he had the chance to wear gaiters laced to his knees.

Thus, three mad folk trudged forth to dig up the past. At least, one mad Englishman and two people who humored him.

Unlike society ladies David did his best to avoid, Sophie didn't fill in the space with inane chatter. No inquiries about his family, how his country estate fared, what he thought about gardening, or Gilbert and Sullivan. She was refreshingly quiet.

Of course, this meant he learned nothing about her. Who was this husband she avoided, why had she decided to hide with Dr. Pierson, why hadn't Pierson mentioned she was breathtakingly beautiful?

He tried not to watch the way she walked, head up, back straight, her skirt swaying. She was a married woman, and not the sort of married woman with whom David had liaisons. That was to say—she was respectable.

Pierson's strides grew longer and more animated as they neared the mounds, he as eager as ever. What he claimed were Roman ruins were little more than lumps in the middle of a pasture. The squire who owned the field, one of Pierson's parishioners, was a patient gentleman who let Pierson dig up his land as much as he pleased, as long as the sheep didn't mind.

The sheep in question, a flock that looked remarkably the same to David year after year, nibbled grass some distance away. Only a few ever strayed to the long mounds, as lusher foliage lay elsewhere.

"Furrows," David said as Pierson squatted down to examine

the long heap of dirt that hadn't changed much since the last time David had been here. "Ancient ones perhaps, but hardly a villa."

"Oh, ye of little faith," Pierson returned. "I found a stone here the other day."

"My, my." David surveyed the vast green land, which smelled of sheep and mud, not the smoke and refuse of London. "A stone. In a pasture. How extraordinary. I ought to have placed a wager with my bookmaker."

"He has a point, Uncle," Sophie broke in.

David tried to hide his pleasure that Sophie agreed with him. "Ah, wisdom speaks."

Pierson creaked to his feet and surveyed them both with pity. "A stone with Latin writing on it."

"Oh." Sophie sounded more interested. "What did it say?"

Pierson spread his arms to make his grand pronouncement. "It said: *Left. Bottom.*"

David raised his brows. "Hardly Cicero, my friend."

More pity from Pierson. "They are builders' marks. The blocks were marked according to the plan so the builders would know which way the walls were put together. The inscription didn't actually spell out the words *left* and *bottom*, but had letters indicating that."

Sounded slightly more promising, but it was David's policy to tease Pierson whenever he could.

"You know those could be stones from a pig's bier or a sheep pen from medieval times. Disappointing to a classicist, I know, but possible."

"Have you ever paid *any* attention to my lectures?" Pierson asked. "A Roman stone and handwriting is vastly different from the medieval. In the middle ages, a builder was more likely illiterate. They still made marks, but often in pictures or simple symbols."

"I beg your pardon," David said, giving him a bow. "I concede your expertise. You found a stone with Latin letters on it. Excellent."

"Quite excellent," Sophie said. "Exciting, even. I am willing to believe in the villa, even if Mr. Fleming does not."

"Did I ever say I didn't believe?" David said, widening his eyes. "I am merely skeptical. Pierson wants to find this villa so much he sees things others do not."

"It only means he is keenly observant," Sophie said. "Where do you wish me to start, Uncle?"

"In that corner, if you'd like." Pierson pointed to earth that had already been raked back. "Don't tire yourself unduly, my dear."

"Do not worry. I am quite robust."

Pierson had taken over a deserted small byre nearby where he stored tools so he would not have to lug them back and forth from the vicarage, and had set up trays for his finds and a table where he could examine them. He unlocked its door, and Sophie dove in, choosing a trowel from the shelves.

Pierson retrieved two spades and held one out to David. "There you are. Have at it, my friend."

David stared at the shovel. "You expect me to dig? Are you mad?"

Sophie was already on her knees, happily jabbing her trowel into the earth. "Perhaps he fears spoiling his work clothes. He seems to prefer to ruin his evening dress instead."

"Of course," David said. "Silk and cashmere are far better for landing on the grass. Actually, when I sought refuge here, I envisioned spending my days in the cozy sitting room with a pipe. Perhaps a brandy at my elbow."

"That wouldn't clear your head." Pierson shoved the spade at him, and David closed reluctant fingers around the handle.

"Good hard work is what you need. And if we find the villa, your name and Sophie's will feature prominently in my monograph on the matter."

"Just the sort of literature my friends peruse," David said, straight-faced. "I'll be famous."

"*I* would be honored," Sophie gestured with her trowel. "Can you turn over this bit for me, Mr. Fleming? Or would you rather pontificate on why you don't wish to soil your working gloves?"

David growled, then drove the spade into the area she indicated with more emphasis than necessary.

Sophie had obviously decided David was a lily-handed dandy who couldn't lift a finger to manual labor. Embarrassing and annoying. David had played rugby at school and still rode and boxed with the best of them. He admitted he affected the lazy persona in order to make people lower their guard with him —politics had turned him into a heinous creature. But there was more to David than met the eye. He was certain of this.

"I begin to understand why your husband suggested you take a holiday from him," he said as he rammed the spade into the soil. "You do have pointed ways of putting things."

Sophie jerked her head up. David regretted the words instantly, and even more when Sophie gave him a fleeting look of naked pain.

Before he could utter an apology, she swiftly turned her attention to the earth and began digging hard, her silence deafening.

CHAPTER 3

*D*avid gazed down at Sophie, his heart banging, realizing he'd just ruined the camaraderie he'd begun with her.

Pierson had moved off and was no help. David knew damn well he'd put his foot into it, but it was hardly his fault. Pierson really ought to send out bulletins on his family members, required reading before visits.

"My apologies, dear lady," David said in his gentlest voice. "I did not mean to give offense. My tongue gets away from me sometimes."

Sophie threw him a glance over her shoulder that was too neutral to be true. "Please dig just there." She continued to jab at the ground, doing no good David could see.

Feeling the invigorating concoction rapidly wearing off, David began to dig, her obedient servant.

Sophie's breath came fast, her hurt too sharp. She

shouldn't mind—it didn't matter—everyone was saying such things. But she hadn't wanted Mr. Fleming to think the worst of her.

She didn't know why his opinion mattered so much—she barely knew the man—but perhaps she wanted her uncle's friends to take her side.

Mr. Fleming began to dig in earnest after his apology, which was abject, she had to concede. Her tongue sometimes ran away with her too.

And why, when she thought about his tongue, did she grow warm inside?

Sophie was finished with men. Once her marriage finally ended, she'd retreat here or to her father's house and live out her life in solitude, perhaps raising sheep or digging up artifacts. Or she'd move to France and join a convent—she hadn't quite decided.

Mr. Fleming's shovel halted. Leather creaked as he sank next to her, the gaiters he'd donned to protect his trousers folding around powerful calves.

"I truly do sincerely and humbly apologize." His voice was deep, full, and his warm breath touched her cold cheek. "I have no business dabbling in other people's marriages. I've come to grief that way before—you'd think I'd have learned."

Against her wishes, faint amusement cut through her misery. Mr. Fleming could drawl an insult one moment and entirely undercut its sting the next by throwing the insult back on himself.

"That's quite all right, Mr. Fleming." Sophie resumed turning over rich loam.

"I'm an unmitigated ass." David put his hand on her wrist, stilling its movement. "I will be in agony until you forgive me."

Sophie raised her head. Her hat caused him to lean out of her way, which he did in a comical fashion.

But what was in his eyes stunned her. She saw anger, intense and heartbreaking, not at Sophie, but at himself. He hated that he'd hurt her, unhappy that he'd given offense to the niece of his friend.

His eyes were that intriguing blue-gray she'd noted before, even more fascinating now that the bloodshot tinge had gone from them. They were eyes that saw much and processed knowledge quickly. A dangerous man ... and a captivating one.

Mr. Fleming was also very handsome. He didn't have the conventional looks her female friends prized—no golden hair or Adonis profile. He was dark-haired with the red highlight she'd noticed before, his pale skin brushed with freckles.

He also had a presence she couldn't grow used to. She had the feeling Mr. Fleming would command her attention whether they were in a ballroom, on a public road, or digging in the mud. That presence sent tingles across her skin and made breathing difficult.

"I said it was nothing," she managed. "I assumed everyone knew of my ... situation."

Mr. Fleming's gaze intensified. "Why? Who is your husband?"

Sophie let out a little sigh. Ah, well, he'd find out sooner or later. "The Earl of Devonport." The name lay thickly on her tongue.

Mr. Fleming blinked once, twice. "Good Lord, you married *Lackwit Laurie*? That damnable little tick?"

Sophie's face grew unbearably hot. "Unfortunately."

"I knew him at school. Unfortunately. Hang on, that means *you're* the Countess of Devonport. The wife he's divorcing."

Sophie swallowed, trying to make her nod nonchalant. "As you see me."

Mr. Fleming peered at her in the blatant way so many gentlemen had once Laurie had destroyed her reputation, no more polite curiosity.

"He wants rid of *you*?" he demanded. "What the devil is wrong with him? Is he blind? Barking mad? Oh, wait, of course he is. He didn't gain the name Lackwit Laurie for nothing."

Mr. Fleming's reaction was more flattering than most, but Sophie tried not to warm to it. She could trust so very few these days.

"According to his solicitors, I am an adulteress—many times over." If she said it quickly, like a joke, it didn't gall so much— almost. "I protested my innocence, but of course, I am a liar as well."

"What does *that* matter?" Mr. Fleming said with admiring astonishment. "If you'd paraded an entire acrobat team through his house and amused yourself with each member, he'd still be a damned fool for putting you aside. If *I* were married to such a lovely woman, I'd look the other away so hard that my head would be on backwards. What sort of poxy bastard would do this to you?" He cut off with an exasperated noise. "Forgive my language—again. I'm not used to guarding my tongue."

"Obviously," Sophie said shakily.

Mr. Fleming grabbed Sophie's trowel and stabbed the dirt repeatedly. "I will just have to speak to Lackwit Laurie."

"No."

The word came out more sharply than she meant it. Mr. Fleming stared at her—he hovered too close.

"I mean, please, do not," Sophie made herself say in a quieter tone. "My name is already in every newspaper, and I'm certain a gentleman dashing in to defend me, however kindly meant, will only make things worse. I would rather remain here at Uncle's until the divorce is finished."

"Hiding away?"

"Yes." Sophie met his gaze. "As you apparently are."

"Touché." Mr. Fleming's lips parted, as though he meant to say more, but he shook his head. "I should have taken *him* to Regent's Park," he muttered.

"Pardon?" Sophie asked, blinking at the non sequitur.

"Nothing." Mr. Fleming dropped the trowel and climbed to his feet, grabbing the spade. "Shall we give up on this furrow and try the next one?"

DAVID DECIDED TO SAY NOTHING MORE TO SOPHIE OR Pierson about Sophie's marriage and apparently insane husband the rest of the morning, but thoughts spun in his head. And schemes. He couldn't help himself—scheming was his nature.

The day warmed slightly, but not much. The exertion of digging, scrambling up and down mounds, and arguing with Pierson heated David's blood and burned out the rest of the alcohol. His body wanted more, but he decided to give it tea instead. Mac Mackenzie had managed to clear himself of all drink, and now imbibed fine-tasting teas he had specially blended for him. Perhaps David would take up his habits.

Easy to have grand intentions when the fit first struck. By the time he sat in Pierson's study that night, Sophie retiring soon after supper, David was happy to accept a goblet of brandy and drink of it deeply.

He regretted the large sip, however, as the sour liquid burned his mouth and choked him on the way to his belly.

"This is foul," he said to Pierson with a gasp. "You ought to let me send you better."

"It is good enough for a poor vicar of a country parish," Pierson answered, taking a modest sip. "Which I am. I like living humbly. A little humility would not go amiss for *you*, my friend."

"Not my fault I was born into the gentry and inherited my father's estates and money." David took another sip, decided it wasn't worth it, and set the brandy aside. His cigar, from the case he always carried with him, was of the finest stock, so he lit that instead.

Dr. Pierson deigned to accept a cigar from him, and soon both men were puffing in contented silence.

"Now then," David said when he couldn't contain himself any longer. "Your niece. Why didn't you tell me she was married to Lackwit Laurie Devonport?"

Pierson gave him a sidelong look. "You never asked. Nor was it your business. He's an earl, so I assumed you knew Devonport. You aristocrats stick together."

"I'm not a peer, only distantly related to one." David sat up straighter and laid his cigar in a bowl. "I did go to school with Devonport, when he was the Honorable Mr. Laurie Whitfield, and I loathed him. Most of my circle did. You should have seen the things Hart Mackenzie did to him, or caused to have done to him. Hart ruled a band of reprobates who'd do anything he commanded. I was one them, naturally."

"Yes, I remember." Pierson gave him a disapproving frown. "I never liked Devonport, and I did voice objection to the match. But Sophie wanted the marriage, as did her mother and father, and so I kept my peace. I'm not certain Sophie was ever truly in love with the man, but she was young and excited, and in love with the hullabaloo that surrounds weddings. So many get caught up in the wedding plans and the gowns and flowers and all the nonsense that they forget what *marriage* means. That the vows are just that—vows. Promises that you'll be true to the other person, their partner in all ways, no betrayals—"

"Yes, yes," David said hastily. Pierson was apt to go on about the lofty meaning of marriage if one didn't stop him, an amusing trait in a bachelor. "What happened? Why isn't Lackwit ecstatically happy that he has a beautiful woman with a saucy tongue and an intellect nurtured by you to go to bed with every night? He objects to her lovers, does he? What reason is that to put aside such a marvelous lady?"

Pierson's eyes took on a glint of anger. "Sophie has no lovers. She is an honorable young woman. The lovers are an invention of Devonport's so he can bring a charge of criminal conversation. He's even persuaded a few of his toady friends to testify in court that they had ..." He broke off and cleared his throat. "You know ..."

"Carnal knowledge of her? Don't be delicate—plain speech is best." David lifted his cigar and took a brusque puff. "Now I am convinced that Devonport's barking mad. For what reason is he so unhappy with that beautiful young woman that he *invents* her adultery? Does she snore? Sing horribly when he's attempting to sleep? Did she try to poison him? Wouldn't blame her there. I'm sorry, but I cannot imagine what sin *she* has committed to cause a man to want to put her aside."

"You believe me that the charges are lies?" Pierson asked in surprise.

"Why wouldn't I? You are the most truthful man I know. And you are not naive about the world, no matter how you hide yourself away in this corner of it. If you say Sophie is innocent, then she is. Besides, I know plenty of women who stray, and you are right—she is not the sort. What I cannot fathom is *why* Devonport wants rid of her. The concoction she made me drink was foul, true, but she was right. It made me feel much better, very quickly. That is no reason to turn a woman out of doors."

"Money." Pierson held his cigar loosely and looked sad. "That is why he is ruining Sophie's life."

David frowned. "Ah. I begin to see a glimmer."

"Sophie had a large dowry, and an inheritance that went to her husband when she married. My sister and her husband were dazzled by Devonport's title and did not make the wisest choices in the marriage settlements."

"And Devonport went through the inheritance," David guessed. "He is extravagant."

"Exactly. The dowry, the money, and the property Sophie held are gone. Now Devonport has his eye on another lady, a widow who is sumptuously wealthy."

"What woman would marry him after what he's doing to his first wife?" David asked in amazement.

"Devonport has cultivated public sympathy for himself at Sophie's expense. They listen to *him*, not Sophie. He is much higher born than she is, and his word carries weight, especially with those who do not know him well. Likely this widow believes she'll soothe him from all his hurts—ladies do like to think they'll be the nurturing angel who heals the misunderstood hero. Plus she'll become the Countess of Devonport and a grand hostess, which must be too enticing to turn her back on."

"There are no children," David mused. "I've never read an excited birth announcement regarding the next little Devonport."

"Another strike against Sophie. She has not produced the requisite son and heir, though they've been married five years. The widow whom Devonport wishes to marry already has two small children—she is obviously fertile."

"Dear God." David felt ill.

Society would consider Sophie lucky to have landed Devonport in marriage. Pierson's family, no matter that Pierson had an amazing brain and much compassion, were inconsequential. Pierson's sister, Sophie's mother, had married a kind nobody—a gentleman with a Cambridge education but no family connections that lifted him above the ordinary. Mr. Tierney had money in a trust from his mother specifically to give Sophie a start, which was why she'd had a fine dowry with a small piece of property attached to it. But though Sophie's father was a respectable gentleman, he had no prominent career, no connections among the ruling class, and no ambitions. So Pierson had told him.

Sophie had gone from nonentity to countess, her husband a peer of the realm and prominent in the House of Lords. Society wouldn't forgive her for betraying this lofty man, no matter what they thought about him personally.

David had mostly ignored Lackwit Laurie since school, because he'd grown from pompous and stupid boy to pompous and stupid man, not worth bothering about. Devonport had never done anything to annoy Hart personally, and so Hart hadn't asked David to ruin him.

But wouldn't it be satisfying to?

"I'll have to run up to London soon," David said, hiding his sudden enthusiasm behind his cigar. "Business keeps marching, even when I'm rusticating. May I presume upon your hospitality and have my room again when I return?"

Pierson's eyes narrowed. "Please stay clear of this business, Fleming. Sophie has had enough pain. I do not want her name associated with yours—that would make things worse for her. No matter how fond I am of you, you know it's true."

David widened his eyes. "Why would you believe me rushing to London to meddle in Sophie's affairs? I've had charges of assault brought against me, and I need to find a barrister to defend me, or try to convince Griffin to drop it, which would be best all around. I do have my own troubles, you know."

"I believe it because I know you," Pierson said. "Leave it alone."

David subsided, or pretended to. "I only wish to help a damsel in distress."

"And I know your reputation with damsels. Sophie is my niece, first and foremost. I realize she is not the sort of lady on whom you usually sate your libidinous nature, or I'd never have allowed you the house, but you do like to manipulate people. For Sophie's sake, please leave it alone."

David raised his hands, the cigar trickling smoke. "I understand. I am to keep my stained paws out of it."

Pierson relaxed, but only a little. "Stay here and help me dig out the villa. It is good to have an able-bodied man to assist me."

"You know, you ought to hire people if you are serious. Let a professional have a look at the site."

"I *am* a professional," Pierson said, wounded. "I have trained in archaeology—did a dig in the Levant, I'll have you know, and one in Northumbria. Found a nice little stash of Viking gold."

"Yes, so you have related on numerous occasions. That means you know people in the business and don't have to force your friends to wallow in the dirt for you."

"But I am a selfish man, and want this find for myself. It's my villa, David. I'll not give it away."

He looked so affronted that David chuckled, feeling better. It had been a while since something made him light of heart.

David also withdrew his statement that he'd rush up to Town the next day. He did need to return to London at some point and seek a defense against Griffin. And while in London, if he happened to look up Lackwit Laurie and beat some sense into him ...

Hmm, he could come up with a much better idea than simple violence. An idea that would destroy Devonport and make Sophie a golden and guiltless angel in the eyes of the world.

He'd need help for that sort of thing, he decided as interest burned through him. Good thing he was friends with such devious people ...

David caught Pierson glaring at him and rearranged his face into innocent lines.

The only man in the world who could stop him was the vicar now regarding him in suspicion. Pierson knew far too much about David Fleming, and David would have to be careful of that.

Mr. Fleming cleared his throat. "Your uncle told me."

Sophie nodded, but her face heated unbearably. "I know."

They stood under a cold but sunny sky next to the furrow they'd begun digging yesterday. Uncle had moved off with his measuring equipment, notebook, stakes, and string, leaving them relatively alone.

"Listening at keyholes, were you?" Mr. Fleming asked in the light tone with which he said everything.

"I did not have to. Your expression when you regarded me this morning was enough."

Mr. Fleming put his hands to his cheeks and moved them this way and that. "Must learn to have control over this face. But is it so bad that I know?"

Sophie kicked at a clod of earth. "The world has split into two camps—one believing I am the greatest trollop in creation and that I have gained my just deserts. The other camp pities me but secretly believes I have only myself to blame. For being a trollop, you see."

"The *entire* world?" Mr. Fleming asked. "Including natives of Tasmania? The Chinese emperor? Trappers in the Canadian forests?"

Sophie didn't laugh. "If they knew of the situation, I am certain they would choose a side."

She studied the soil as she turned it with her boot, head down so she wouldn't have to look at Mr. Fleming. As it was cold this morning, she'd donned a fur cap rather than a hat, so she had no brim to keep him at a distance.

"There is another camp," Mr. Fleming said. "Those who believe your innocence."

"A very small camp." Sophie dared raise her head. His gray-blue eyes were fixed directly on her—most unnerving. "Uncle. And me. Even my parents, while they are kind, aren't certain. My husband is so very convincing."

"You forgot me," Mr. Fleming said in a quiet voice. "*I* believe you."

Sophie flushed, unable to meet his assessing gaze. "Why should you? You barely know me, except through Uncle."

"He is one reason. His opinion counts for much. The other is that I know something of your husband, Lackwit Laurie, the Dunce of Devonport. Devonport will do anything to get what he wants, with a directness that's alarming. Likely how he convinced you to marry him in the first place. I can't imagine anyone actually falling in *love* with him."

"I thought I had," Sophie said, though she was amazed at herself now. Laurie had been attentive, flattering, even fawning, and Sophie, too often a wallflower, had fallen for him.

"He does have a certain oily charm, I suppose," Mr. Fleming

mused. "And women believe him handsome. But then, a few ladies think *I'm* handsome, so there is no accounting for taste."

Sophie looked straight at him, her inhibition fleeting. He had the gift for making her relax her guard. "Are you fishing for a compliment, Mr. Fleming?"

His eyes widened. "Me? Good Lord, no. I am stating facts. Your unctuous husband has now charmed a rich widow into throwing in her lot with him. Hopefully someone will talk her out of it before it's too late ..." A smile spread across his face, lighting his eyes and driving out the shadows. "Hmm."

"What are you thinking?" Sophie asked in alarm. "You look very much like a snake just now."

"Damn my expressions. I can't keep anything from you. I am thinking nothing, dear lady. Wheels simply spin in my head without my permission. You will be well rid of Devonport in any case. Good Lord, his name sounds like a piece of furniture. You might as well be Lady Writing Desk, or Sophie ... let me see ... Sofa."

Sophie sucked in a breath and dropped her gaze again, frantically wishing the villa would reveal itself at her feet and swallow her.

"Oh, devil take it." Mr. Fleming put gentle fingers under Sophie's chin and raised her face to his. His eyes held anguish. "They do call you the last one. Bloody bastards—bloody ingrates. I did not know, I promise you. It's only the wheels, you know ... not in my control."

"It is a natural association," Sophie said faintly. "I cannot blame you for making it."

"Yes, you can." He slid his fingers away, leaving a chill where he'd touched her. "I always strive to be the cleverest man in the room. It is why I am a bachelor. Your uncle chooses that life, but I am alone because I'm an uncouth idiot. I loved a woman once. Only once. She crushed me like an eggshell."

"Oh, dear." A spark of interest slid through Sophie's unhappiness. "Is that true? Or are you trying to make me feel better by being more heartbroken than I am?"

"No, it is perfectly true. She'd tell you herself, and she'd tell you exactly why she threw me over. I'd have driven her mad if I'd married her, and she knows it. Her husband is my closest friend, so it makes things a bit awkward. For me, I mean—the two of them pity me but are not bothered in the slightest that they are deeply in love and happier than most people ever dream of being. To them we are all comrades, chums for life."

"Poor Mr. Fleming. I had no idea you were a tragic hero."

"Ugh." He grimaced. "Never say so. I prefer to think of myself as a strong rock, solid in the stream of life, unbothered by the slings and arrows of outrageous fortune."

Sophie couldn't help her smile. "*Tragic hero* explains things much better."

"I am devastated, dear lady. Now, I believe we are supposed to be looking for a Roman villa. Your uncle will march back here and demand to know why we haven't yet uncovered a fabulous wall painting."

Sophie held her trowel out to him. "Go to, Mr. Fleming."

Mr. Fleming eyed the muddy ground with distaste. "He must wield highly magical powers, your uncle. He has forced two perfectly respectable people into grubbing about in the loam, and we still *like* him."

Sophie's laughter bubbled up and spilled over. She hadn't laughed in true mirth in some time, and it felt fine, like being washed clean.

Mr. Fleming's absurd expression drained away until he

looked at her without his mask in place. His face had lost color, making the faint freckles stand out across his cheeks.

Naked emotion filled his eyes, a self-deprecation that approached self-loathing. This was a lonely man, rejected by the woman he loved, forced to watch her love another. He'd fled here —Uncle said because he'd been arrested, of all things—needing peace. Like Sophie.

Mr. Fleming touched her cheek.

She flinched, but only because she hadn't been touched in such a way in so long a while. Not with this tender inquiry.

Mr. Fleming immediately lifted his hand away, but when Sophie held his gaze and did not move, he touched her again.

His fingers were gentle, gloves smooth, warm with the man beneath them. He brushed her cheek then drew one finger down and across her lips.

Sophie swallowed. After her husband's accusations, gentlemen had tried to corner her, believing they'd be welcome. But their awkward attempts at groping were worlds away from Mr. Fleming's touch.

He traced her lips, floating his thumb across the lower one, pressing its cushion. He followed what he did with his eyes, lashes flicking as he studied her mouth.

The cold wind pushed at her, but Sophie paid it no heed. Mr. Fleming's fingertips stroked heat deep inside her, a burning in her veins she'd never felt in her life, no matter that she'd shared a marriage bed with her husband. She'd never felt this heat, never knew the join of her legs could grow so hot and damp.

Their point of contact was the merest touch, but at the moment, the only thing in Sophie's world.

Glide, brush, caress. He moved to her lips, her cheek, lips again. He'd shaved today—his skin was smooth, plus she'd heard curses from the top of the house when he'd nicked himself. She smelled his shaving soap, the leather of his gloves, the mint-infused water he used to sweeten his breath.

So careful of his appearance today, when the first morning at her uncle's table he'd looked and smelled like something from the gutter.

Wind tugged at Mr. Fleming's clothes, as it tugged at Sophie's. Tiny cuts marred the skin beneath his chin, attesting to the fact that he was unused to shaving his own face.

He pulled his gaze from her lips and met her eyes squarely. "You," he whispered, "have exquisite beauty."

Sophie could barely breathe. She was incandescent, light as a balloon. The merest breath of wind would take her away.

Mr. Fleming lowered his hand, removing his beautiful touch. He studied her another moment, then his brows came together, his expression darkening.

"Damnation," he snarled. "Damn everything to hell."

He turned on his heel and marched away, sinking his polished boots into mud as he went.

CHAPTER 4

*F*our days. David shook his head as Pierson goaded him out into the field yet again.

Four days he'd endured life with Pierson, rising at a hideously early hour in the morning to tramp with the man to dig in the pasture. Returning in the late afternoon to a hearty meal prepared by Mrs. Corcoran, lively conversation, games in the evening, then a snifter and cigar with Pierson before turning in.

A staid, organized, quiet existence. The only strong drink David consumed was a small glass of wine at supper and one goblet of brandy as he and Pierson conversed after Sophie went to bed.

Four days of gazing at Sophie across the breakfast table, carrying her tools to the dig, watching her and Pierson play draughts in the evenings and Sophie nearly always winning. Pierson played like a shark, so her victory meant something.

Days of being near Sophie and not near. He'd touched her in the cold field, the satin softness of her skin coming through his thin gloves. She'd stood very still, like a wild animal giving him leave to touch her.

Four agonizing days of keeping himself away from her, pretending to view her as the niece of his old friend, a sweet young lady forbidden to a man like David.

This would kill him.

Pierson was correct that Sophie wasn't the usual sort of woman David chased. David had liaisons with the most elite courtesans in the world, ladies who were companions to kings. Or, aristocrats' wives, bored with the endless round of balls, plays, masquerades, and musicales, their husbands off with their own mistresses. They sought David for amusement and diversion.

Sophie, with her sleek black hair and fine green eyes, her gentle manners and spirited banter, was far too pristine for the likes of David Fleming. Her husband might have decided to ruin her, but in truth, Sophie was a well-bred and virtuous young woman, the sort mothers pulled quickly out of David's path.

He had to sit near her every night, walk with her every day, and keep his hands—and his craving, and his words—to himself.

David told himself that he wanted her for the novelty of it. Perhaps because he was isolated here, and she was the only female company in view. He was lonely, and Sophie was pretty and agreeable.

But it was nothing pretty and agreeable that made David wake in the night in his tiny room, hot and hard, stifling a groan. Sophie was beautiful, like a naiad—ethereal and elusive. She had wit as well as knowledge—she'd read more books than David had even heard of. She easily matched David's barbed speeches with retorts that put him in his place. He was enchanted.

More than that—he'd wake in a sweat from erotic dreams where Sophie surrounded him, her long hair spilling across his bare chest and aroused cock. The groans that dragged from his mouth came from frustration, desire, and brutal yearning.

He'd throw off the blankets and try to revive himself by plunging hands and face in a basin of cold water. In the morning he'd descend, eyes burning and skin itching, and there she'd be across the breakfast table, chewing toast and smiling serenely at him.

He had to leave.

David decided on the fourth day that it would be his last. He'd return to London, deal with Griffin and his prosecution, humbly asking Hart for assistance if necessary. That and apologize to Eleanor for not responding to her summons. He'd now recovered sufficiently to face her.

"Shall we try here?" Sophie said when they reached their now-familiar trench that morning, gesturing with her trowel.

The earth was pockmarked with holes, as though all the ground-dwelling animals in Shropshire had dug their burrows in one place. The deepest holes had been made by David, he taking out his frustrations by driving his shovel into the soft dirt.

He swung his spade from his shoulder and pounded it into the ground where Sophie indicated. If only she didn't have such lovely hands even her thick gardening gloves couldn't hide.

"Not so hard," Pierson admonished as he passed them on the way to his trench. "Roman craftsmen built these villas with care, not for you to destroy with your carelessness. Flinders Petrie advocates slow exposure, sifting each layer and recording what is found with precision."

"Yes, Uncle," David said, so meekly that Sophie laughed at him. He loved her laugh.

Pierson ignored him and returned to his trench.

"He works so hard," Sophie said as David resumed digging, more moderately this time. "I hope he finds something, one day."

"He has a bee in his bonnet," David said. "But he's no fool.

There must be *something* buried here, even if it isn't a Roman villa."

"Wouldn't it be fine to uncover it for him? Whatever it is?" Sophie knelt and started carefully troweling through the hole David had begun. "It might take some time, but time is something I have in abundance. I believe I shall grow old looking after Uncle, helping him turn up bits of the past."

David didn't answer, his breath not working well. He ceased digging and leaned on the spade. "I'm leaving for London in the morning," he announced abruptly.

Sophie's eyes widened. She wore her white fur cap pulled down over her ears, black curls protruding from beneath it in a most fetching manner.

"Leaving?"

David nodded, ignoring the lump in his throat. "I have barristers to consult, charges of attempted murder to thwart. Well, one charge. The irony is that I'm innocent of this one."

Sophie stared at him without blinking, then she rose to her feet, wind catching at her skirt. "When will you return?"

David hesitated. "I don't know if I will."

"Oh."

The swallow that moved her throat gave David some hope she cared whether she saw him again. Not that it mattered. Sophie was in an awkward situation, and David pursuing her would only make it more awkward.

He hadn't exaggerated when he said he needed to fight the murder charge. A letter from his solicitor had found him—his solicitor knew every place David took himself off to whenever he fled London. The solicitor had informed him that Griffin continued to claim David had shot at him and wanted him to stand trial for it. Only the influence of Hart and Detective Superintendent Fellows kept the police from making David await the trial in Newgate.

David had other things he wanted to pursue in London as well, but he knew he'd be unwise to tell Sophie and Dr. Pierson about them.

Sophie fixed him with an unreadable green gaze. "We will miss you."

"Will you?"

She studied him as she had when he'd daringly touched her a few days ago, unable to stop himself. Courageous, unswerving. Beautiful.

"Of course." Sophie shook herself and turned away, sinking to her knees on the tarp she'd spread across the damp ground. "Uncle enjoys your chats in the evening, and I enjoy winning our draughts games."

"Draughts, chess, cards, puzzles, riddles ..."

He liked the smile she shot him. "Your own fault for not paying attention. Though I imagine a game of Pope Joan is not very exciting to a man used to the card tables at White's."

"My dear, the company at White's is ghastly. Any game can be exciting if the stakes are right."

"Matchsticks?" she asked impishly.

"I'll have you know, I hoarded those matchsticks like gold until I had to turn them all over to you and your uncle. You two are such sharps, you could form a syndicate and fleece the multitudes."

"Yes. Such a pity Uncle is a vicar."

David relaxed, happy to hear her teasing. He'd miss it ...

No, this was for the best. He should leave now, before it became more difficult. If he didn't go, he'd linger, let his solicitor and Hart take care of Griffin, hope Sophie grew so fond of him she wouldn't mind if he enticed her to his bed.

His bed, which at the moment lay in a tiny space below the ceiling beams in her uncle's house. David mentally cuffed himself. He was an idiot.

Sophie reached into the hole she'd been sifting through and delicately retrieved a small pebble. "This is pretty."

David, interested in spite of himself, leaned to look. Sophie brushed the mud from her find and held it up.

What little February sunlight leaked through the bank of clouds winked on a fragment of blue stone, rendering it translucent. The edges were jagged, a piece broken long ago.

Sophie unfolded to her feet, ignoring David's hand, which he'd instantly thrust out to help her. "What do you suppose it is?" she asked, eagerness in her voice.

David peered at it, but it remained a piece of stone to him. "Who knows? Broken vase? Glass from a farmer's ale bottle?"

"One this blue?" Sophie turned and waved at Pierson. "Uncle! Come and see!"

About twenty yards from them, Pierson calmly set down his measuring stick and got to his feet, dusting off his knees. He tucked his notebook under his arm and walked to them, betraying no anticipation. He'd been disappointed so many times about this villa, David supposed he'd grown stoic.

Sophie scrubbed off the stone with the handkerchief David lent her. Polishing it brought out more of the deep blue color, the piece almost glowing, but it wasn't glass.

Pierson studied the fragment that lay on Sophie's palm. He poked at it, then he picked it up and turned it this way and that with professional detachment.

David saw when his eyes lost their resignation and took on a gleam of excitement. And then triumph.

Dr. Lucas Pierson, the learned, unruffled man who'd taught

David that there was good in most people if one looked hard enough, suddenly leapt into the air and let out a yell.

"I knew it!" Pierson landed again, his boots splattering mud. "I knew there was a villa here! Take *that*, British Museum. And *that*, Antiquarian Society." He punched imaginary foes with a balled-up fist. "My dear niece, you are a *genius!*"

"Mr. Fleming dug the hole," Sophie said generously. "What is it, Uncle? Part of an amphora? Or a bit of jewelry?"

"No, no, nothing so staid. This is a piece of tile." He opened his hand. "See how it is so precisely cut on this side? It is part of a mosaic, probably from a floor. No army hut would have mosaics on the floors. This is part of a larger building, like a bathhouse, or a villa."

David felt his heart beating faster, a smile pulling his mouth, as though he'd single-handedly discovered the remains of a Roman palace.

"You believe there's more down there?" he asked, Pierson's enthusiasm contagious.

"Somewhere." Pierson spread his hands and waved them over the mounds. "A beautiful floor, walls painted in glorious colors, a heating system ..."

His voice grew more animated with each word until he leapt into the air again. He came down and ran off across the green with the lightness of a man half his age.

"I did it!" his voice trailed back to them, and then loudest of all, coupled with another jump—"*Eureka!*"

David and Sophie burst out laughing. Her eyes were alight, her nose pink with cold. She was vibrant color in a sea of gray, a glow in the endless twilight of David's life. They stood very close, the moment of discovery and elation warming the air between them.

CHAPTER 5

*D*avid's mouth was hot, skilled, strong. The air was frigid, but Sophie knew only David's warmth, the bulk of his body shielding her. His fingers pressed her cheek, much as they'd done a few days ago when he'd softly touched her.

He didn't command or possess, didn't demand Sophie respond. He simply kissed her. She tasted the coffee he'd drunk this morning, felt the scrape of whiskers his razor had missed.

The space between them filled with an energy that brushed Sophie even through layers of fabric. She parted her lips and leaned into him, hungry. She hadn't realized how hungry.

David started as she rose to him, but then he took her mouth in a deeper kiss, his tongue finding hers. The hot friction made Sophie's knees buckle, but David's strength held her steady.

Her mouth was stiff, her return kiss clumsy. She was out of practice, and she'd never been kissed like *this* before.

David didn't seem to notice, or care, about her lack of expertise. He had enough of it for both of them. His kiss caressed, gave, was all about pleasure. He knew how to touch, to draw forth fire.

Sophie no longer used the formal *Mr. Fleming* in her mind.

He was David, had always been for her, but Sophie hadn't been able to admit it.

His thumb pressed the corner of her mouth, opening her to him. He cradled her head, her hat sliding sideways, curls loosening from their pins.

Sophie craved the kiss, David's warmth, himself. He was another lonely being crying out, and Sophie responded with eagerness.

She closed the fraction of space between them to seek the greater warmth of his body and slid against him, David so tall. Sophie rose on tiptoes, tilting her head so she could continue the kiss.

His arm came behind her, and she felt herself bending back as David slid one hand up to cup her breast through her thick coat. A tingle of fire raced from nipple to heart, and Sophie let out a moan of need.

In the next moment, she stumbled, David's embrace gone. She clutched at her hat and righted herself with difficulty, dragging in a burning breath.

David's eyes were wild, like stormy skies. He'd lost the tweed cap he'd donned against the cold, and his hair tumbled in the wind.

"Damnation." His voice was cracked, the self-loathing blatant.

"David ..."

"No." David took a hasty step back, narrowly missing the hole he'd just dug. "Don't speak to me. Don't even *look* at me."

"David." Hurt cut through Sophie's haze of elation. "I'm not an innocent miss fresh from my debut."

"Aren't you? As near as. Bloody hell."

He darted a worried glance behind them, but a quick look

told Sophie that Uncle Lucas was still dancing around, waving his arms, celebrating his Eureka.

"No need to swear at me," Sophie said, her heart pounding. "I am my own woman. I may kiss whom I please."

"The devil you may. If any other man kissed you like that, I'd kill him. I'm near to strangling myself with my own hands."

"Don't say such things." Sophie's eyes widened in alarm. "Not even in jest."

David backed another step. "Very well, I'll horsewhip myself instead. But I'll do it in London. Good day, Miss Tierney."

He grabbed the cap that had fallen to the wet grass and jammed it on his head, then turned his back and walked away.

Sophie wanted very much to run after him, wrap her arms around him, demand that he stay, beg him if she must. To behave like a needy and wanton woman, pleading for his touch.

If she did so, she suspected David would throw her off and keep marching. She'd have to watch him go, he so obviously regretting the kiss.

Sophie's loneliness, hurt, and rage at Laurie for his nastiness, for his rejection, welled up until it burst. She'd been priding herself on keeping her emotions well hidden, but David's kiss had loosened them, and her fury poured forth like a pent-up geyser.

"Blackguard!" she shouted. "Run away. Desert your friends. I don't care."

David turned, his anger just as high. "I *am* a blackguard. Tell your uncle I am gone."

"Tell him yourself." Sophie paused. "Do you mean you are leaving for London *now*?"

"On the moment." David resumed his swift walk, heading across the fields to the road.

"Do you intend to march all the way there?" she yelled after him.

"To the train." He gestured ahead of him. "In the village."

"The village is that way." Sophie pointed in the other direction.

"Damnation." David glared where she indicated and began to stride on that course.

"What about your things?" Sophie cupped her hands around her mouth. "Or shall I have Uncle throw them out the window?"

"He can chuck away whatever he likes." David didn't slow, continuing his stride toward the village, out of her life.

"Go then," she shouted. "I hope I never see you again, you horrible man!"

His only response was a wave.

David's tall figure blurred into the landscape as Sophie's eyes filled with hot tears. Her breath caught on a sob, and then she let the tears come, weeping until her body shook. There was none to see her cry but the sheep and the rabbits, and they didn't seem to mind.

THE SMOKE. LONDON WAS APTLY NAMED, DAVID REFLECTED as the train carried him past belching chimneys under a dark gray sky.

In February the town was full, the social and political season having well commenced. Men shouted at each other in the neo-Gothic Houses of Parliament, and hostesses sparred with politicians' wives at soirees and supper balls that were as much about power as any debate in the Houses.

David at one time had reveled in the game. He'd been on his feet in Commons, shouting down his opposition during the day, seducing the opposition's wives at night. David was a prime player, with his own circle of toadies, at the same time he was

Hart Mackenzie's right-hand man. He and Hart had torn up Town between them. Not much had happened in London without their knowledge and say-so.

Or so it had been. David knew his days of scheming with Hart as they consumed cigars and whisky in the presence of elegant and skilled ladies were past. Hart continued to harass his foes in the House of Lords as Duke of Kilmorgan but now went home to his wife and children to bask in domestic bliss.

Not that Hart's wife wasn't the grandest hostess in Britain. Her gatherings were designed not only to assist Hart with his machinations but also to delight and astonish. Eleanor's parties were legendary.

David had been avoiding her gatherings lately, as he'd been avoiding everything else in his life.

He descended at Euston Station and took a hansom south and along the Strand to the Temple. In Middle Temple, in a tiny square called Essex Court, David rang the bell of a neat house. He had an appointment and was readily admitted.

Not long later, he sat in a comfortable chair sipping excellent whisky and facing a tall Scotsman with very fair hair and penetrating gray eyes.

"Doesn't look good for you," Sinclair McBride announced. "Griffin is raging about you all over London. His uncle is calling to have you detained in Newgate, though we have persuaded him that you are under house arrest in Shropshire." Sinclair's gaze sharpened. "Yet, here you are."

"Things to see to." David reclined lazily, sipping Mackenzie malt Hart and Ian supplied to Sinclair, as the man was now part of the family. "People to look up."

"Your solicitor should be here—at all meetings you have with me," Sinclair said firmly.

"Hated to bother the old chap. I keep him busy enough as it

is. So, you will defend me? Even though your practice is mostly prosecution?"

"I take defenses that are in a good cause." Sinclair looked David up and down, clearly not considering him a good cause.

David spread his arms. "I am completely innocent. Griffin fired at *me*. I was willing to ignore the entire incident, but he is a fathead."

Sinclair sank back into his chair, taking up his glass of whisky. The strain and grief of his former life had entirely gone from the man, David was pleased to see. Sinclair's home was now quite happy and filled by his delightful wife and four tumbling children—hellions, every one of them, including the wife, lucky man. David was quite fond of the swiftly growing Andrew, a fearless boy who reminded David of himself at a young and adventurous age.

Sinclair's domestic happiness had made him an even more talented barrister—he had declined a judgeship offered to him in order to stand in the courtroom and win case after case with aplomb. The Scots Machine, other barristers called him. The criminals called him Basher McBride, for his unflinching zeal in putting away bad men. Exactly the sort of barrister David needed on his side.

"Your solicitor is interviewing witnesses," Sinclair said. "Though a statement from you would be helpful. More than *I didn't do it*. I need the entire story."

"That *is* the entire story." David swung his booted foot. "Griffin fired his weapon and missed, thank God. I never fired mine. We were all roaring drunk at the time."

"Griffin had injuries," Sinclair pointed out with his glass of whisky.

"From my fists, not my pistol. I had injuries as well."

"The fight was about ...?"

David grimaced. "A woman. What else? Griffin is convinced I was bouncing upon his lady wife, but I was not. She might have cuckolded him, true, and I wouldn't blame her. But it was not with me. He and I have been sparring for years, however—verbally, I mean, on the Commons floor. I've thwarted many of his stupid schemes."

The supposed affair with his wife was only the excuse, David knew, for Griffin to release his frustrations. Griff was a touchy bastard, especially when his lack of political acumen was thrown in his face. Accusing David of attempted murder must be his way of trying to remove David from his path once and for all.

Sinclair tapped his fingertips on the glass. He made no move to write notes, but David knew Sinclair did not have to. He had an amazing brain.

"I'll do what I can for you," Sinclair resumed. "Eye witnesses would be useful, but I believe putting Griffin on the witness stand will be best. I have the feeling his testimony won't hold up to my questioning."

David chuckled. "Not under the lash of Basher McBride, it won't. Why do you think I told my solicitor to hire you?"

Sinclair gave him a thin smile. He was the best barrister in London but too modest to accept praise. Many a hardy criminal wilted under the stare of the Basher.

David took a sip of whisky and the two descended into companionable silence. David hadn't needed to come here to talk about his defense—his solicitor could have done that. *Had* done it, in fact.

"By the way," David said when his glass was nearly empty. "What do you know about the Devonport divorce?"

"The Devonport case?" Sinclair asked in surprise. "That's in the civil courts. I only go after dire villains."

"True, but you must know something about it."

Sinclair bent him a wary look. "You've been out of London a long time if you haven't seen the newspapers. The journalists are excoriating both husband and wife." He shook his head, a flicker of sympathy in his eyes. "It's a bad business."

"I only read the sporting news. Life is difficult enough without journalists constantly flogging us with the horrors of the world."

Sinclair gave him a sharp stare, the one that penetrated a man's skull and tore out all his secrets. "What is your interest?"

"I happen to know the wife in the case," David said, trying to sound nonchalant. "She's the niece of a dear friend."

"Is she?" Sinclair's gaze didn't waver. "Interesting."

"You know, you put more insinuation into three words than most men put into entire speeches. I will say about her what I do about myself—she didn't do it."

"Devonport *is* going a little far in his accusations," Sinclair said. "He's claimed his wife committed open adultery. Two men so far have come forward to testify that they were her lovers, but Devonport says there are many more. I might believe one or two, but knowing what I do about ladies of society, I'd say she did not have time for more than that."

"And I say she did none of it."

David slammed down his glass, and the remaining liquid leapt over the rim. He pictured Sophie's sweet smile, her green eyes looking straight into his. No coyness or falseness about her.

He dragged in a breath. "Trust me, McBride, I know women who have no inkling what the word *fidelity* means, and I know mostly innocent women who've had a single illicit affair in their lives. The former ladies have a complete lack of guilt, the latter have too much of it. Sophie—Lady Devonport—is unlike any of them. She did *not* have affairs with these men, no matter what Devonport claims. He wants rid of her so he can marry a wealthier woman. If I actually do shoot anyone, it will be *him*."

Sinclair listened with his uncanny perception. "I see."

"So I've come to you for help."

A glint of understanding entered Sinclair's gray eyes. "And I would enjoy helping Lady Devonport—her husband is a foul man. But as I say, the case is in the civil courts. Devonport's barristers are in Lincoln's Inn."

"Aha, you know which barristers then? Do you know them personally?"

"Yes." The answer was cautious.

"Then cajole them. I want an appointment to see Devonport. I'd simply go to his secretary and ask, but Devonport hates Hart, and me by extension, and I'm certain the secretary would have a standing order to refuse me. But if Devonport's barrister suggests it ..."

He left it at that. Sinclair was canny—he'd invent something to get David inside Devonport's house.

Sinclair gave David the barest of nods. "I will see what I can do."

David knew then that his admittance was guaranteed. They did not call Sinclair the Scots Machine for nothing.

———

HIS SECOND MEETING OF THE AFTERNOON WAS TRICKIER. David didn't have an appointment for it, but he turned up and took his chances.

Hinch, his coachman, drove him to Grosvenor Square and halted outside a tall house, as he had the morning David had fled to Shropshire. This time, David was sober, bathed, shaved, and decently dressed. He gazed up at the intimidating house, but today he was eager to rush inside and sit before the one woman in all London he knew could assist him.

At one time, David had run in and out of the Mackenzie mansion as he pleased, as Hart's friend and confidante, but these days, he made sure to send in his name and wait to be announced. Hart's haughty majordomo admitted him and led him up the grand staircase to a sunny room the Duchess of Kilmorgan had commandeered as her own.

Eleanor's touches were everywhere. Haphazard stacks of photographic plates lay on every flat surface, along with open books on photography and botany, astonishingly beautiful photos of flowers, and many pictures of her two sons and husband.

The mechanical aspects of photography had progressed so that these days a person no longer had to sit motionlessly in front of a camera on a tripod, waiting in stiff agony until the shutter closed. Eleanor had the latest in photographic apparatus at her disposal, and she shoved these cameras constantly into the faces of her nearest and dearest. The results were scattered over the top of the piano—she'd caught her sons laughing, shouting, grinning, and hugging their dogs.

David lifted a framed photograph of Hart—Hart was dressed in this one, fortunately—gazing down at his youngest son, Malcolm.

The picture was amazing. Hart the formidable Scotsman in tartan kilt, the man feared throughout Parliament and the cabinet, smiled down at his son, his hard face soft, his love for the little boy apparent. Eleanor had caught him well.

"One of my best, I think." Eleanor's voice sounded at David's elbow. "Hart growls like a bear about me shooting everything in sight, but I can't help myself. And my husband is so very photogenic. He does not mind, really, but he doesn't want to be seen as vain, so he tries to deter me."

"Dearest El." David returned the picture to its place to squeeze her hands and kiss her cheek. "I am pleased to see you so happy."

"Happy and distracted." Eleanor gently withdrew her hands, a faint smile on her face. "Young Alec is at school this year as you know, and my heaven, he can find scrapes to get into. Not always his fault, though he could avoid them if he truly tried, but he is kindhearted and apt to take things in hand for another's own good, and then it all goes wrong. Hart, of course, thinks his son should be a model of propriety and angelic sweetness. How he can have that idea, I do not know, because you recall better than most what a hellion Hart was at school. Besides, the model of propriety is never liked—we were horrible to the prissy head girl at Miss Pringle's Academy. She still is awful, poor lady. I saw her the other day—"

"El," David said firmly. He'd learned from Hart long ago that the only way to stop Eleanor when she began full steam was to break in forcefully. "I do need your help on a matter."

"Well, of course. Sit down, my dear fellow, and tell me all about it. I heard you were rusticating with Dr. Pierson. How delightful. Or perhaps it is deadly dull. Which are you finding it?"

Eleanor led David to a set of couches that faced each other, low-backed, comfortable affairs upholstered in cream and yellow. No more heavy carved furniture in dark horsehair for the duke and duchess.

David sat obediently, marveling that he could study Eleanor's wisps of red curls and very blue eyes without the pang of regret that had filled him for years. At the moment, she was simply a friend, one whose assistance he greatly needed.

He launched into his tale without preliminary and outlined

his plans. Eleanor listened with flattering attentiveness, and when David finished, laughter lit her eyes.

"Oh, that is perfect. You are the most devious man I know. How splendid." She leaned forward with conspiratorial eagerness. "What do you wish me to do?"

CHAPTER 6

Sophie sipped her tea in her uncle's study two days after David had departed. Uncle Lucas had his feet up near the snapping fire, a brandy in his hands, resting from his frantic work at the dig.

He'd barely ceased his labors to conduct church services, running in at the last minute to throw on vestments for evensong, morning prayer, and the main service on Sunday. Fortunately the parishioners were very low church and expected little more than a reading of the service, a few hymns accompanied by Mrs. Plimpton on the wheezing organ, and a gentle sermon.

Uncle peppered most of his sermons with analogies to antiquities from long-lost civilizations, but the villagers, used to his obsession, didn't mind very much. Or so Sophie heard from Mrs. Corcoran. She had not yet summoned the courage to attend church with her uncle.

"Will you tell me about Mr. Fleming?" Sophie ventured.

Uncle opened the eyes he'd closed and gave her a keen stare. Instead of asking about her curiosity, he launched straight into an explanation. "Fleming is a reprobate and a scoundrel, but a good-hearted man. I had much hope for him when I was his tutor at Cambridge. But alas, he chose the path of darkness."

Sophie warmed her hands on her teacup. "If he has such a bad reputation, why have I heard nothing about him?"

Uncle crossed his slippered feet on the ottoman and took a slurp of brandy. "Because your parents shielded you well. His name would never be mentioned to a debutante, and you'd never be allowed to a gathering he attended. On the other hand, David has done much work—behind the scenes and admittedly by being a manipulative villain—to relieve the poor, improve conditions for factory workers, and other numerous reforms he will forever deny."

"Why should he deny them?" Sophie asked in bewilderment. "If he's helped people."

"Because he *likes* to be seen as a reprobate—and he is." Uncle gave her a dark look. "He achieves his goals by means it's best not to examine too closely."

Sophie studied the dregs of her tea, a few leaves floating in the bottom. "He told me he'd fallen in love with a woman and that she broke his heart. That she was now his closest friend's wife."

Uncle nodded. "Indeed. He was head over heels for the Duchess of Kilmorgan—Lady Eleanor Ramsay at the time. She was being arduously courted by Hart Mackenzie, before he became duke. Lady Eleanor refused Mackenzie's proposal, quite rightly, I thought. Mackenzie was not the finest of men then, and believed he could have anything he wanted without question. David, poor chap, was potty about Lady Eleanor, but willing to step aside for Mackenzie. When Eleanor threw Mackenzie over, David thought he could easily step into the man's shoes, but he later told me he hadn't realized Eleanor's very deep love for Hart. Lady Eleanor did not regret her choice to jilt Mackenzie, but she was not interested in substituting another for him. She retreated to her father's house near Aberdeen and became his assistant, housekeeper, gardener, bottle-washer, and David had to leave her be. He was in agony over it for a long while, poor chap."

"I know the Duchess of Kilmorgan slightly," Sophie said, trying to hide her discomposure at the tale. David had obviously loved Lady Eleanor more intensely than his glib words had let on. "She has little to do with me, because her husband despises mine. They are on different sides of the wall that is politics."

"And that gulf will never be breached," Uncle said decidedly. "Which is why I chose the clergy, though that can also be fraught with political peril. Give me a country church and a simple life. The bishops can enjoy fighting in the House of Lords all they like."

"Did David—Mr. Fleming—never marry? Or court any other?"

"No." Uncle gave Sophie another piercing look. He might prefer the life of an unsophisticated country vicar, but he was uncommonly wise. "Fleming is a captivating young man, my dear. I know this—I have been captivated by him for a very long time. But his charm is tarnished. He and his father quarreled mightily days before his father's death, and that haunts him. Fleming fears he caused his father's illness—which is nonsense, of course—and mourns that he had no chance to reconcile with him before it was too late."

"Oh, how sad," Sophie said in genuine sympathy.

"David took it to heart, yes. But do not decide that he turned into a libertine because of it. He was one long before that, and he has always enjoyed being unconventional and shocking. Whenever the Duke of Kilmorgan wishes to defeat an opponent, he asks David to bring out the dirt on that person and hound the unfortunate man until he surrenders. Morals fly out the window. David is ruthless."

Sophie swallowed. "I see."

Uncle softened his voice. "I refuse to shield you from the truth, my dear. As much as I love him, David Fleming is not a respectable gentleman. I allowed him to stay under this roof with you because I know he pursues only ladies of questionable virtue, which you are not. In spite of what others are currently claiming about you, you are innocent and he knows it. He has an instinct."

Except that David had kissed her like a storm and then raged at himself for it. Sophie's heart stung when she thought of the kiss —the imprint of which she even now felt on her lips.

He had taken her mouth in hunger that matched her own. David might believe her innocent of her husband's accusations, but he had kissed her like he would a lover.

"The Duchess of Kilmorgan has never been a lady of questionable virtue," Sophie pointed out, her throat tight. "Yet Mr. Fleming fell in love with *her*."

"She was the exception." Uncle nodded. "I knew Fleming would come to grief over her, but he would not listen to me. Never does. He is a chap who needs to find things out for himself, even if it half-destroys him to do so. I keep hoping that someday ..." Uncle let out a rueful breath and shrugged.

"You hope he'll become the man you see deep inside, and make you proud," Sophie finished. "But people won't always be what we want them to be." She trailed off, pain filling her heart.

Uncle sent her a look of sympathy. He understood that Sophie had wanted Laurie to be the man of her dreams, but the dream had never come true. The day Sophie realized that her ideal husband and the real Laurie were worlds apart—when she'd found out about his string of mistresses, including a few of her own maids—was the day her marriage had died. She'd fallen out of love with Laurie long before he'd decided he wanted to rid himself of her.

"Fleming will discover who he is someday," Uncle said. "Or he will not. Not everyone achieves a happy ending."

"Including me." Sophie sighed. "The question is, what do I do now? The divorce has already ruined me, and it is a long way from being final yet. I do have one idea, but I must have your approval."

"Yes?" Uncle, who'd started to drift into a contemplative state, gave her his attention again. "Tell me this idea."

"I'd like to become your assistant, if you'll have me." Sophie spoke rapidly, before she lost courage. "You've told me much about your digs and I know how to take notes and make sketches, how to measure, how to notate the finds. Between the two of us, we should be able to reveal this Roman villa, and then—who knows? Go on to excavate more sites in Britain, perhaps. Or you can return to the Middle East, as you've always longed to. I'm not afraid of a little dust or sunshine."

Her uncle listened, eyes lighting. "That is true. I'd love to try my luck in Palestine. There's the ruins at Masada ..." He gazed off into the distant past before dragging himself back to the present. "Of course, my dear, you are welcome to stay here and help with this dig. An excellent scheme, and a good way for you to gain experience. You will be my secretary—I always need someone to go over my articles and get the punctuation correct. Though I must warn you ..."

His expression turned dire, and Sophie stilled, worried.

"Mrs. Plimpton has the rheumatics, and she's complaining about difficulty playing the organ. Says she wishes to retire. So you might be recruited to plonk out the hymns on a Sunday."

Sophie relaxed. "Oh dear. Are you certain your parishioners will let the Whore of Babylon into their church? The walls might fall down."

"No one believes you the Whore of Babylon, child," Uncle said kindly. "Truth to tell, the parishioners rather like having a scandalous person in their midst. It gives the village a certain cachet."

Sophie knew her uncle was trying to make her feel better, and she was grateful. She smiled. "Thank you, Uncle."

"You are very welcome, Niece."

Sophie sipped her tea and said nothing more. As her uncle's assistant, she could leave off finery and begin to wear dowdy frocks, becoming a dried-up woman with no interest in gentlemen without delay. Playing the organ in the church loft where no one could see her would only hurry the process along.

This would be her life, then. Safely hidden from the world, buried in excavations and typing up Uncle's notes into something coherent, perhaps earning a footnote in his monographs thanking her for her help. She no longer had to worry about what life would bring. It would be mapped out for her, unchanging.

Sophie imagined what David would say to her thoughts, pictured his wry look, heard his cynical laughter. She clutched her teacup and barely stopped her tears.

THE EARL OF DEVONPORT OCCUPIED A TALL HOUSE IN Portman Square, very Georgian, with columns, a fan-lighted door, and a lofty entrance hall. The earl received callers in a study on the first floor, at the top of a flight of stairs designed to inspire awe.

The house had escaped the ruthless modernization of

David's generation, retaining its early nineteenth-century faux Greco-Roman simplicity. The cool white walls, busts of great men of history, and elegant furniture came as a relief from the noisy, crammed, choking city outside.

The decor was likely the result of Laurie's father's tastes. Lackwit Laurie Whitfield would hardly have the understanding, let alone the interest, to maintain such understated luxury. That is, unless Laurie had drastically changed.

No, no, David assured himself. He decidedly had not. Any man who would throw away Sophie Tierney on a whim had proved he was a complete dolt.

The Earl of Devonport rose from behind a desk when the majordomo ushered David into the study, the timing calculated to imply that David had interrupted perusal of very important letters.

"Fleming." Laurie dropped the papers and came around the desk as the majordomo withdrew. "Such a surprise. Or shall I call you Devilish David? A long time since our silly days at Harrow, what?"

David clasped Laurie's extended hand, noting the grip was firm. So was Laurie. He'd changed from pudgy boy in short pants to muscular man in a trim black suit, though he'd never have height or be rid of his bulbous nose—but he was striking. Lackwit had learned how to make an impression.

"Fleming is fine," David said when their hands parted. "Or D.D., if you prefer. I could call you L. L."

Lackwit Laurie burst into laughter, a deep, mature sound. "Ah, yes, the puerile nicknames we gave each other in school. Boys can be so cruel. You don't have sons yourself, do you?"

David shook his head. "Lifelong bachelor, me."

"Too bad, old man. Domestic bliss has its place."

He waved David to a chair. David took it, letting his gaze go to the bookshelves around him, which were filled with erudite tomes. "Domestic bliss, eh? Aren't you charging through courts to obtain a divorce?"

Laurie waved that away and resumed his seat behind the desk. "Only because the woman I chose decided to hurt me in the most scurrilous way. Fortunately, I have met another lady who will make me very happy."

"How lucky for you." David's gaze rested on a book on the nearest shelf. "Erasmus Darwin. Interesting. His translation of Linnaeus changed botany as we know it, do you not think? And he was far ahead of his time in his opinions on the education of women."

Laurie's brow furrowed. "Never knew he was interested in women. Can't agree with him that men are descended from monkeys. He simply met too many monkeys when he traveled around the world, I wager. Loneliness and wishful thinking, more like." He snorted a laugh.

"Mmm." David forbore to explain that, while related, Erasmus Darwin and Charles Darwin were two different people, the younger born several years after the elder, his grandfather, had died. "As interested as I am in natural history, my visit is of a different nature."

"Yes, indeed. Why have you come? Does the Duke of Kilmorgan want my backing on one of his daft bills? He'll never win us over, no matter how many Highland dances he performs. Tell him to go back to Scottish-land and eat haggis." Another snort, Laurie fond of his own wit.

David again decided to keep silent, this time on the fact that he too was Scots and preferred beefsteak and vegetable soufflé to sheep's innards.

"My request is of a more personal nature," David said, draping his arm comfortably over the back of the Louis XV chair. "I have a favor to ask, man to man, one Harrow boy to another."

"I remember you and Hart being great bullies at Harrow," Laurie said. "To me, I mean. Well, to most not fortunate enough to be in your circle."

"As you say, boys can be cruel." David spread one hand. "Males are thoughtless at that age, without the learning, experience, and gentler sentiments we acquire once we become men. I can only apologize."

Laurie gave him a nod, a smug one. He'd obviously thought David had come to grovel, to beg the condescension of a lofty earl.

The thought of this man touching Sophie made David's blood boil, but he held himself in check. He could only accomplish what he needed by remaining cool-headed.

"What is this favor?" Laurie asked the question with the air of a man who could make one's dreams come true or shatter them in a blow.

"Miss Tierney. Your wife."

Laurie frowned. "You mean Lady Devonport."

"What is in a name?" David smiled as Laurie looked befuddled at the question. "You see, my dear fellow, I am slightly acquainted with Miss Tierney. She is the niece of an old friend of mine. This friend is most distressed for her."

"You know my wife?" Sudden rage crossed Laurie's face. "Good Lord, have you come to offer your testimony of crim con as well?"

David pretended to look puzzled, tamping down his desire to punch Laurie's protruding nose. That Laurie instantly believed David had tumbled Sophie increased the boiling inside him.

He kept his tone calm. "You mean have I had criminal conversation with Miss Tierney? No, no. You misunderstand me.

I barely know the gel. But my friend, he was like a father to me, and I hate to see him unhappy. I am here to ask, on his behalf, for you to give up the divorce."

Laurie blinked. Not what he'd expected. Laurie settled into his chair, which he'd half risen out of, looking thoughtful. "I am sorry your friend is distressed, but I have already begun the proceeding. My wife, sadly, is an adulteress. I have two of her lovers willing to appear in court and say so."

David came out of his slouch and sat forward, changing from old acquaintance begging for a favor to the man who would take charge of the room.

"Now, old chap, you and I both know Miss Tierney is nothing of the sort," David said. "The gentlemen who are testifying to the crim con are friends of yours, paid handsomely for their efforts. Their reputations will not suffer too much, and they'll be rewarded for coming to your aid. I know all this, because I've spoken to them, and both confessed everything to me." Sinclair and Eleanor had many connections, and had helped David make appointments besides this one.

Laurie flushed, uneasiness settling upon him. "Does it matter? My marriage is at an end. If the dear laws of England would let me finish it without all this mess, I certainly would."

"Yes, declaring 'I divorce you,' three times and tossing her out of your tent would be much easier."

"Quite." Laurie clearly did not understand the reference, just as he had no idea what was inside any of the books in this wonderful library. "But I must take my wife to court, or I will not be free to remarry."

"And that is the crux of the matter, is it not?" David pinned Laurie with a gaze worthy of Basher McBride. "You wish to marry another. I understand that. Therefore, you must legally end your current marriage. But have you not thought of annulment? There will still be legal papers to wade through, but annulment is much less scandalous. You and Miss Tierney have no children to worry about, is that correct? None to become suddenly illegitimate when the marriage is declared invalid?"

"No sons, no." Laurie scowled. "No offense to your friend, but his niece never came up to scratch in that way."

David raised his brows. The rage inside him danced about, seeking release. He had already decided how to let it out, in a way it would be most effective, but it was difficult not to simply grab Laurie and bang his face into his desk.

"Really?" David drawled. "Or is it that your little man isn't up to the task?"

Laurie's expression went dark. "Of course that is not the case. Why would you even suppose such a thing? When children don't come, it is the woman's fault. Childbearing is up to them."

David could put forth plenty of medical arguments to prove Laurie wrong, but he let the statement pass. "So, no children whose lives you will ruin. Then why not annulment?"

"An annulment is not such a simple thing," Laurie said impatiently. "To declare a marriage invalid is difficult. There are certain conditions that must be met. Trust me, I looked into it."

"Yes, I do imagine your solicitors with their heads together day and night scheming, scheming. Let me see, if I recall, the conditions are ..."

David paused as though trying to remember, but he knew damn well what they were. Sinclair had gone over the process of annulment with him meticulously, but David was more interested in what Lackwit Laurie knew.

"One is if we are too closely related," Laurie finished for him. "I studied our family trees, and Lady Devonport and I are not even remotely connected." He looked disdainful. "Her family is far inferior to mine, which I should have noted long before she dazzled me."

David barely refrained from spitting at him. He touched his fingers, counting off. "Very well, then. That possibility has been wiped away. Next?"

"That we have already contracted a previous marriage. I had not." Laurie pressed his hands to his chest, a virtuous man.

"What about Miss Tierney? You could not find a marriage in her past—or at least, invent one?"

"I thought of that." Laurie looked regretful. "But claiming she married another before me—that would have to be proved."

"Yes, I can see it would be ticklish. You'd have to produce documentation, witnesses, perhaps the vicar who performed the service. Even if Miss Tierney had married on the Continent, a judge here would want to send for the documents there."

"I say, why do you keep referring to her as *Miss Tierney?*" Laurie looked affronted. "She is still my wife, at least legally, for now."

"Because if you annul the marriage, as I believe you can, she will never have been the Countess of Devonport. Therefore, her true name is Miss Tierney."

Lackwit had to work through that. "I see."

"Let us resume—Miss Tierney is not a close relation. Nor is she currently married to another. I would choose the next point on which a marriage can be annulled—insanity—on your part, I mean—but alas, that also would require testimony. And Miss Tierney was of marriageable age when you wedded—too many witnesses to that." David touched his last finger, unable to hide his glee. "But I believe another reason for annulment is ..."

"What?" Laurie said irritably. "We have run through them all. Except ..." His face went red as he realized where David was leading him.

"Yes, indeed," David said, and pronounced the word with satisfaction. "Impotence."

"On her part, yes," Laurie snapped. "But still, it is—"

"No, no, old chap. You mistake me," David interrupted in a hard voice. He smiled into Laurie's face, a cold, angry smile. "Of course I mean the impotent one is *you*."

CHAPTER 7

*L*ackwit Laurie stared in such bafflement that David couldn't hold in his laughter. The man's resemblance to a stuffed fish at the moment was hilarious.

Laurie coughed. "But I am not ..." He held his fist to his mouth and wheezed. "You know."

"Flaccid as a deflated balloon?" David suggested. "Limp as a drowned worm? Are you certain?" He made a show of glancing about the room. "I see no sons or daughters crawling around your house. No by-blows from your mistresses. I've investigated this point. Are you certain *you* are up to scratch, old son?"

"Of course I'm not impotent!" Laurie's voice rang out. "What the devil are you playing at?"

"You could pretend to be. To obtain the annulment."

Laurie was up from his desk, advancing on David. David made a show of taking his time to rise to meet him.

"You two-faced blackguard!" Laurie snarled. "You're her lover, aren't you? You want me to back off so you can have her. Well, I refuse." He stepped to David, putting himself nearly nose to nose with him—not difficult as Laurie's stuck out so far. "There will be no annulment. I will divorce her and cover her with so much muck, even *you* will be disgraced if you take her. You've tipped your hand, my friend."

David's gaze was steady. "You always were a bit slow, weren't you, Devonport? An annulment will save you reams of cash. Why do you care what your wife gets up to after that? You will have no blemish on your character and can marry whom you choose."

"What the devil are you talking about? I can't make a case for *impotence*." Laurie flinched at the word. "Such a thing must be proved, and it never will be. Please, do your worst. Send a lovely courtesan or even a homely midwife to come to me and touch my prick. It will bounce forth in all its glory and your impotent theory will be dust."

"An excellent idea." David pretended to brighten. "I will make a bargain with you. If a lady can get you stiff—and she agrees to bear witness to a judge that you're flowing like a virile man—I will withdraw the idea. But, if she proves we should change your name to Limp-Prick Laurie, you will have your marriage annulled, announce to the world that Miss Tierney was falsely accused, and go your merry way. Your wealthy widow might think twice about marrying a man who can't please her in the bedchamber, but that is the risk you'll have to take."

Laurie stepped back, his smile huge and disquieting. "You have made a bad choice, Fleming. I will accept the bargain and enjoy squashing you. I'll have Devilish David in court as one copulating happily with my wife, and be damned to you—and to her."

David raised his brows. "*Devilish David* doesn't have the sting of *Lackwit Laurie*, does it? Or *Limp-Prick Laurie* as I will call you from now on." David stuck out his hand. "I believe we have an agreement. I will send my solicitor to draw it up formally if you like. Then you will ... er, you know ... be put to the test."

"I look forward to it," Laurie said in hearty tones.

"I dare say."

David and Laurie shook on it, Laurie trying not to hide a wince as David strengthened his grip. David turned away, taking up the walking stick he'd leaned on the chair and making for the door.

"You're a bloody fool." Laurie always did have to put in the last word. "And I shall prove it."

David continued into the hall. "There is a reason we call you Lackwit, you ass," he muttered.

"What was that?"

David turned back, raising his voice. "I said, I wish you good day, old sass."

Laurie nodded stiffly. "And you."

David grinned as he went down the stairs, his steps light. He took his hat and greatcoat from the footman, slinging them on as he ducked out into the pounding rain, whistling a merry tune.

———

SOPHIE DECIDED THAT KNEELING IN THE MUD, HACKING AT A mound of dirt, was no bad thing. In the last few days, she and Uncle had turned up a few more loose tiles, one black, one the brilliant red of heart's blood. A floor lay somewhere under here, Uncle Lucas vowed.

As impatient as he was, Uncle would not simply plow down until he found it. Modern archaeology was not a treasure hunt, he declared, but a search for knowledge of the past. Even so, Sophie knew Uncle longed to find his villa before he grew too elderly to enjoy it.

She sat back on her heels, glad of the tarp that shielded her from the worst of the muck, and wiped her brow. More to do before teatime.

A movement across the field caught her eye, and Sophie froze, a clod of earth dropping from the trowel to her skirt.

He'd said he wasn't coming back. Had shouted it. Sophie climbed stiffly to her feet, heart pounding as the unmistakable form of David Fleming tramped toward her. Dismaying how quickly she'd learned his walk and way of moving.

Uncle Lucas dropped his spade and rushed forward, peppering David with delighted greetings. Sophie remained where she was, as though the mud cemented her feet in place.

"Thought you'd disappeared for good, my dear fellow," Uncle Lucas said as he and David moved toward Sophie. "Leaving me to wonder when you'd turn up again."

"Like a bad penny." David's self-deprecating drawl cut through the wind. "Found your villa yet?"

"More pieces of it." Uncle Lucas tried and failed to hide his excitement. "Sophie is most clever at discovering relevant bits. She is officially my assistant now, so treat her with respect. Also compassion for putting up with me."

"Excellent." David rested his gaze on Sophie, his gray-blue eyes holding a heat that had nothing to do with his polite words. "I am certain she will do far better than anyone else you allow on your dig. Including me."

Sophie warmed to the sincerity in David's words, but she suspected he was thinking, as she was, about the kiss. At least, *she* was picturing the kiss with intensity, her lips burning as though he'd just lifted his mouth away.

Then again, he was a libertine, Uncle had told her. David must kiss ladies and walk away from them all the time. He might have already forgotten their spontaneous embrace.

She realized both men were staring at her, awaiting her response. "It is very good to see you back," she blurted. *Oh dear, like a besotted schoolgirl.* "Uncle missed you, though he does not like to say so."

Uncle Lucas sent David a sheepish grin. "I might have let on that I enjoy having you about."

David gave him a mock bow. "You flatter me, sir. I shall be certain to return often—you are good for my pride."

Uncle shook his head in despair. "One day you will learn to gracefully accept a compliment from your friends. I say we adjourn for tea. We've done enough here today, and the weather is turning colder."

Clouds had blotted out the sun and now a fine mist began to fall, coating grass, earth, the tarp, and the three humans foolish enough to be out in it.

David stepped to Sophie and offered his arm. "Miss Tierney? Shall I see you home?"

He had a strange insistence on calling her Miss Tierney, not that Sophie minded. She'd never quite believed herself as the Countess of Devonport, and she soon would no longer be.

She wished Uncle had cut in to escort her, but he only waited, looking pleased at David's politeness. Sophie closed her fingers on the crook of David's arm, her knees going shaky at the strength beneath the wool. She'd end up flat on her face if she weren't careful.

David said little as they tramped back to the vicarage. Uncle Lucas kept up a stream of talk about the dig and his speculations, never inquiring what David had been up to in London or why he'd returned. Sophie said nothing at all, not trusting herself to speak.

Not long later, they gathered around the table in the warm dining room. Mrs. Corcoran brought out a lavish tea of sandwiches, scones, soup, and divine cakes, not seeming to mind that they'd come in early. Sophie's curls were still damp from hurried ablutions in her room—her haste to wash off her grubbiness and rush back to David unnerved her.

He sat across from her now, as he'd done the first morning of his stay. Today his dark hair was neatly combed, the red in it imperceptible in the gloom of the afternoon. His suit looked new, fresh from the tailor, a long frock coat and loosely tied cravat which were the height of fashion.

After maddening civil conversation—dissecting the weather, the slowness of certain trains, the thick pall of London—David turned to Sophie, color brushing his cheeks.

"A bit of good news for you, Miss Tierney. Lackwit Laurie— the Earl of Devonport, that is—will no longer be pursuing a divorce. Or at least, I predict he will decide this within the next week or so."

Sophie had plucked up a piece of sponge cake from the tray. At his words it fell from her numb fingers to the tablecloth, a puff of icing sugar bursting from it like white mist.

"Oh." Her fingers remained in the air, unable to move. "How ..."

This should be the finest news she could wish for. No divorce meant no trial, no gentlemen standing before a judge swearing they'd been her lovers. Her reputation might continue to be smeared by the rumors, but not destroyed by the certainty. A divorced woman never recovered from the shame.

She swallowed as Uncle Lucas and David watched her keenly. A shadow outside the doorway told her Mrs. Corcoran was avidly listening.

"A divorce is a terrible thing," she said in a choked voice. "But on the other hand, I no longer wish to be married to my husband. It would mean I'd be free."

Free to hide in her uncle's house or follow him across the world, wherever the fit took him. She might be unwelcome in polite society, but she'd be free nonetheless.

If Laurie no longer sought the divorce, she'd be trapped as his wife forever. She'd be his property, subject to his commands, his malice ...

David closed his fists as he registered her dismay. "No, no. My dear, Miss Tierney, forgive my idiocy. I am telling it wrong. He and his solicitors will decide to *annul* the marriage rather than go through the procedure of divorce. You'll be free and clear of him but without the humiliation of the trials."

"Annul?" Sophie wet her lips, the word tasting strange. "Laurie will never do that. He cannot—there are no grounds."

David smiled like a fox who'd just outwitted a pack of the best hounds. "I believe you will soon receive a paper that says you are Miss Sophie Tierney and always have been."

He was too serene, too prideful. Sophie narrowed her eyes as her heart began to pound. "What did you do?"

"Me?" David pressed a hand to his chest. "Why should I have anything to do with it?"

Sophie gripped the edge of the table. "You disappear to London and claim you won't return, then you pop up again announcing that my marriage will be annulled, when neither my husband nor his solicitors have ever mentioned any such possibil-ity. I can't help but think this is down to you."

"Exactly." Uncle Lucas fixed him with a stern gaze. "Explain yourself, my boy."

David lifted his teacup, glanced at the tea inside, then set the cup down and pulled out a silver flask. "I thought you'd be pleased." He dolloped whisky into the teacup and tucked away the flask.

"I asked you not to interfere," Sophie said in a hard voice. "Begged you, as I recall."

"As did I," Uncle Lucas put in. "Your name attached to Sophie's will cause her even more scandal."

"Worry not, my friends." David sipped his doctored tea. "My name will not come up in this business at all. I *do* know how to go about these things. Please do not tell me you'd prefer a divorce, dear lady. An annulment is embarrassing, of course, but nothing that won't blow over."

"I will be ruined all the same." Sophie's cheeks went hot. "If the marriage is declared invalid, I will have been living with a man not my husband."

Sharing his bed, she meant, but could not bring herself to say. Not that Laurie had touched her after the first few years of their marriage. When Sophie hadn't conceived, he'd sought entertainment elsewhere.

David wore an odd smile. "I don't believe so. You might be the object of pity, but you'll weather it." He had a smug gleam in his eyes, very pleased with himself.

Sophie wasn't certain whether to laugh, scold, or throw up her hands and flee the room. She chose to remain quiet, retrieve the fallen sponge cake, and put it out of the way on a plate.

The discussion was nonsense, in any case. David could not change the world, or Laurie, no matter what he thought. There were no grounds for annulment, and the divorce would continue. Laurie was a spoiled man and would have his own way.

The situation was impossible, even for someone as canny as David. All she could hope was that he hadn't made things worse for her.

She lifted her teacup and glared at David over it. She refused to be a namby-pamby chit in front of David about all this. She'd secured her future as Uncle's secretary, and she'd have a fine time.

His look turned puzzled at her resolve, but he shrugged and lifted a profiterole—a puff pastry bursting with cream—and took a bite, cream sliding across his lips.

"Mmm." David closed his eyes as he swiped up the cream with his tongue. "You've outdone yourself, Mrs. Corcoran," he called out the open door.

"Go on with you," Mrs. Corcoran's good-natured voice floated back.

Sophie couldn't move as David drew his tongue over his lips, licking the cream into his mouth. He opened his eyes to look directly at Sophie, and her blood burned.

She glanced quickly at Uncle Lucas, but he'd become absorbed in his notes on the dig while absently shoving cakes into his mouth.

David swallowed. "These truly are most excellent."

He smiled across the table at Sophie, challenging her. He expected her to wilt at his sensuality, she realized, to fall under the table at his feet as she suspected many women did.

Blasted man. Sophie snatched a profiterole from the three-tiered tray and quickly stuffed the whole thing into her mouth.

A mistake. Cream gushed from her lips, and Sophie coughed. She snatched up her napkin and coughed into it, her face scalding. Silly Sophie, choking on a puff pastry to show a gentleman she cared nothing for him.

David was off his chair and around to hers, pounding her on the back. Uncle looked up from his notebook in concern.

Sophie wiped cream from her mouth and tears from her eyes. "I am well." Her voice was a hoarse gasp.

David dropped into the empty chair next to her, his warmth too close. "Are you certain? Cream puffs can be deadly."

Sophie patted her mouth with the napkin. "Don't be absurd."

Uncle, seeing she was truly all right, went back to his notes with a chuckle. "Deadly cream puffs, indeed."

"Try another." David plucked one from the tray. "A small bite. They are quite delicious."

What did he wish from her? For her to make a fool of herself? Well, she was capable of that without his help.

Sophie snatched the profiterole from David but this time made herself take a delicate nibble.

The cream, thick and sweet, smeared her mouth. David's gaze flicked to it, smile gone, as Sophie licked it away.

She felt heat on her lips as though he'd licked her himself. Her whole body smoldered as his focus remained on her mouth. Sophie carefully took another bite.

David's stare held fire, intensity, fierce desire. Sophie clutched the profiterole, cream oozing to her fingers. She absently put her forefinger to her lips and sucked the fingertip clean.

David let out a ragged breath and rose abruptly to his feet. "If you will excuse me, Pierson, Miss Tierney. I need a walk."

Without waiting for their response, he strode swiftly from the room. He called more thanks to Mrs. Corcoran, then the front door slammed, and his footsteps faded down the slate path outside the house.

Uncle raised his brows but said nothing, returning to his notes. Sophie took another shaky bite of her cream puff, her confusion and the memory of what had been in his eyes blazing inside her.

"I am quite enjoying this," Eleanor said as she sorted through plates of the photos she'd shot that day.

"You do love photography." Her husband, the lofty Duke of Kilmorgan, lounged in a nearby chair, cupping a glass of Mackenzie malt. The windows were dark, night and London fog sealing them into their warm nest.

"Not what I mean. I meant—"

"I know exactly what you meant," Hart rumbled. He leaned back in his chair, a Mackenzie plaid kilt draping his legs and woolen socks. Eleanor liked him this way, rumpled at the end of a long day, his reddish hair awry, his golden eyes warm and half closed. "You are talking about David and your promise to help him be devious. Have a care, El."

"Nonsense, it is most entertaining being devious. Mrs. Whitaker is a brick, is she not? I imagine most gentlemen never realize how very clever she is."

"Oh, they know." Hart let out a chuckle. "Or discover it too late."

"And she is subtle. Knows exactly how and when to strike —rather like you and David. She's very kind to help, when she doesn't even know Miss Tierney. I ought to have taken Miss Tierney under my wing long ago, but Devonport is on the other side of the fence from you. Politics is a stupid thing."

"True." Hart shrugged. "But it is better than tyranny."

"Tyranny *is* politics, you know, just of a different sort." Eleanor studied a photo of young Malcom and a cat on its hind legs, smiling at the image. "Anyway, I have decided I will make a friend of Miss Tierney and see that she does well. David sets quite a store by her."

She became aware of Hart's piercing gaze. "How do you know that?" he asked in suspicion. "Did he say so?"

"No, indeed. But why else would David be churning that marvelous brain of his to set her free of her awful marriage? I have a feeling David regards Miss Tierney as much more than the pitiable niece of his mentor."

Hart listened in growing consternation. "El—as I said, have a care."

"I think it's marvelous. David has been alone far too long."

"My love, David Fleming is never alone. He is surrounded by people day and night, especially *night*. Believe me, he does not suffer by himself in a monk's cell."

"Don't be maddening. I did not mean *alone* in the literal sense. I mean in his heart." Eleanor lightly touched her chest. "He needs a wife."

"God help us." Hart took a long sip of whisky. "Would ordering you to cease your matchmaking tendency do any good?"

"Of course not." Eleanor abandoned her photographic plates and went to him. Hart's eyes softened as Eleanor curled up on his lap and rested her head on his formidable shoulder. The tension between them changed, from husband and wife disagreeing to the electric awareness that flowed from Hart to Eleanor and back again. "David is your best friend. He's performed monumental tasks for you over the years. Do you not wish to see him happy?"

"You are boxing me into a corner." Hart's voice vibrated her pleasantly. "If I tell you to leave off, you'll accuse me of not wanting David to be happy. I *do* wish him well, but that does *not* mean I condone you rushing him into matrimony with a lady he barely knows."

"Then we must see that he learns more about her." Eleanor ran her fingers down the placket of Hart's open shirt. The warmth of the man beneath enticed her, but she made herself not touch him except through fabric—far too distracting. "They may not suit at all, but we must give them a chance."

"We," Hart repeated. "You keep saying *we*."

"Well, of course. David trusts you."

Hart growled. "Not if I shove him at a woman and tell him to marry her. He'll think I've lost my mind."

"He is already interested, if he is giving the problem this much thought. You must see that. But we will be careful, as you insist."

"I see you've already decided." Hart lifted Eleanor's hand, scattering her thoughts by kissing her fingertips. "What do you want me to do?"

Eleanor blinked. "I must say, you agreed very quickly. I thought I'd have to do much more persuading."

Hart's relaxed manner vanished, and the dangerous man she'd fallen in love with surged to the surface. "I never said I'd not command a price."

"Ah." Eleanor sank into agreeable warmth. "When will I have to pay this price?"

"Not *when*. For *how long*." Hart's golden eyes glittered. "We are starting now."

"*We?*" Eleanor slanted him a coy look.

Hart growled. He came off the chair, Eleanor in his arms, his strength breathtaking. Eleanor knew they would not make it to their bedchamber, but the rug before the fire was plenty soft. Plans, and photography, could wait.

SOPHIE WASN'T SPEAKING TO HIM, DAVID CONCLUDED. AT least, not in the easy, friendly way she had before.

She was furious, and David felt it with every glance. The February chill the next day as he returned to the dig with them was nothing to her coolness.

What had he expected? David chided himself as he shoved his spade into the earth. For her to swoon into his arms?

Sophie had entreated with him not to interfere, and he'd ignored her plea. For a good cause, David told himself. He wanted to save her from humiliation and utter ruin.

In London, his choice had been clear. Here at the vicarage, David had to face himself with honesty. Had he put plans in motion to unselfishly help Sophie or did he have visions of her melting before him in undying gratitude?

Damnation. The problem with being friends with a vicar was that his ethical ideas started rubbing off, no matter how hard David tried to avoid such things.

Yesterday, when Sophie had stuffed the profiterole into her mouth, cream exploding across her lips, his entire body had gone hard. Even more so when she'd nibbled the second bite. Droplets of cream had clung to her lips, begging David to kiss them away.

When she'd sucked the cream from her forefinger, he'd been swamped by a vision of her in a fire-lit bedchamber, delicately catching cream from the pastry on the tip of her tongue. In this vision, Sophie hadn't been wearing a stitch of clothing, a coyly draped bedsheet making her all the more enticing.

Fleeing into the cold garden had been his only choice.

David pulled up his shovel and turned to Sophie, the iciness emanating from her nettling. She knelt on hands and knees on a tarp, skirts primly hiding her ankles as she skimmed her trowel through the dirt, utterly ignoring him.

"You were angry when I left for London," he said to the hat that obscured her face. "It seems my return has made you even more so." He waited, but there was no response. "Would you like me to leave again?" His voice was a touch louder. "Or would that also irk you?"

Sophie lifted her head, her face chiseled beauty in the shade of her hat. "I have no interest in what you do one way or another, Mr. Fleming."

David rammed his spade into the ground. "So you say, but your eyes are shouting at me to go to hell."

"Truly? I had no idea my eyes were so loud."

David held up his hands, palms facing her. "I have offended you, enraged you, annoyed you, infuriated you—I know that. But I had the best of intentions, I promise."

Sophie climbed to her feet, hand tight on the trowel. "I dare say you did, but you likely have made things worse. My husband will *never* agree to an annulment. And now that he knows the notorious David Fleming has a friendship with me, he will be all the more vicious." She waved the trowel as she spoke, scattering dribbles of dirt.

"You could trust me to know what I am doing," David said impatiently.

"*Why* should I? I know so very little about you. My uncle is fond of you, which, so far, is the only point in your favor."

To hide his sudden hurt, David pressed a dramatic hand to his forehead. "Ah, lady, you grieve me. Have I not behaved like a perfect gentleman?"

"No." Sophie folded her arms. "You've flirted with me, kissed me, confused me, gone behind my back to do precisely what I asked you not to, *and* enticed me with a profiterole."

David's laughter bubbled up along with his treacherous imagination. "Fickle woman, you have kissed *me* and plunged me into the deepest bewilderment. You are furious with me no matter which way I turn, and I believe you tried to confound *me* with a profiterole. Most alarming when you nearly choked on it."

Sophie's face reddened, and she pointed with her trowel. "I believe you ought to dig in another part of the field, Mr. Fleming."

"Pierson directed me to dig *here*. And here I stay."

"Well, he told *me* to dig here as well."

"Then we are at an impasse."

Sophie glared. David wanted to laugh his triumph, but at that moment, Sophie stooped, came up with a damp clod of earth, and threw it at him.

Mud thwacked his coat, brand new from his tailor, made for the messy business of archaeology. It was the best Scots tweed.

"Bloody hell, woman." His snarl was also the best Scots, his years of Harrow, Cambridge, and flitting through the top of London society flowing away.

Another chunk of mud hit his midsection. Sophie's fury had segued into merriment, her eyes gleaming satisfaction.

Oh, she wanted to play, did she? David tossed aside the shovel. He bent and gathered mud into his gloved hands, sending her an evil grin. He liked that Sophie's eyes widened in trepidation, but he'd be gentle with her. Perhaps.

He took a quick step toward her ... and found himself falling, his feet penetrating a deep hole. The balls of mud fell from his hands as he windmilled for balance and found none.

David toppled slowly forward. He braced himself to land facedown, but as he hit the earth, it opened up and swallowed him whole.

CHAPTER 8

avid!" Sophie shrieked. She unfroze from the horror of watching David fall through the earth and dashed to the spot where he'd disappeared. "David!"

Bogs could drown a person while they thrashed in desperation. The thought of David, a man so full of life, being dragged out of sight forever streaked terror through her.

Sophie reached the edge of the square hole David had fallen through and sank to her knees, heart thudding. She spied his body, facedown at the bottom of a shallow cavern, weak sunlight barely illuminating the interior. David lay unmoving, wet earth around him, but he'd landed in a damp cave, not a bog—thank heaven.

He didn't move, didn't groan. Sophie hiked up her skirts, caught the edge of the hole, and dropped down to him.

She landed on stone covered with dirt and had to stoop to hands and knees under the low roof. "David," she whispered frantically.

"Music ..."

Sophie scrambled to him, uncertain she'd heard right. "David, are you hurt?"

"Lady, thy voice is music." David rolled himself over with difficulty, his face scratched, his words hoarse. "Is this heaven?"

"If it is, it's cold, dark, and damp and half a mile from my uncle's house. You *are* hurt." Sophie cupped his cheek, brushing away earth and blood with her gloved thumb.

"Heaven," David said with conviction. "And music. Look."

He repositioned himself on all fours and swiped dirt from the floor.

A painted eye stared back at them. Its pupil was a rich brown, the lid pale ivory lined with black lashes and one black arched brow.

"Good heavens." Sophie gaped then helped David brush away more grit and mud to reveal once-smooth tile. "It's a mosaic."

She understood in a moment why David had gone on about music. He revealed part of a lyre, being plucked by the person with the keen brown eye. More frantic rubbing revealed another figure, smaller and female, with a flute.

"Orpheus," David said excitedly. "Master of music."

"Not necessarily," came a voice from above. The opening darkened as Uncle peered down at them. "Could simply be a chap playing at an entertainment, flute girls at his side." The dry tone left Uncle Lucas and he clasped his hands in joy. "My dear fellow, you've found my *floor*."

"No, indeed," David said. "Sophie had been diligently digging at this spot while I was vagabonding. I only widened the hole. With my body."

Sophie had to grin. "You could say he stumbled upon it."

David's eyes began to sparkle. "I dropped in, and there it was."

"You un*earth*ed it. Needing no shovel."

"No, indeed," David said. "It was a bodily blunder."

Sophie laughed, the sound echoing strangely in the close hole. David's smile was warm, genuine—happy.

The expression transformed his face, erasing the tired disdain, revealing David the man. Decadence fell away to make him more handsome than ever, never mind the abrasions on his cheeks.

His smile faded as he and Sophie studied each other, but his mask did not drop back into place. Sophie lifted her hand to hover near his hurt face.

David quickly glanced at the opening, which was light again, Uncle having vanished. "He's gone very quiet up there."

Sophie jerked her hand away and scrambled to her feet, careful of the mosaic. When she stood up fully, her head reached just above the hole. "Uncle?"

Uncle Lucas had fallen to his knees, his hands pressed together in prayer. A tear trickled from his closed eyes.

"Are you well, Uncle?" Sophie asked softly.

David rose next to her, his body and hers close in the narrow opening. His warmth both comforted and unnerved her.

Uncle Lucas opened his eyes, his face wet, a smile beaming. "I was thanking God for his guidance, and asking forgiveness for being so excited about earthly pleasures." Uncle climbed to his feet, brushing mud from his knees. "My dear friends, this is a wonderful, wonderful thing. Thank you for making an old man's dream come true."

"ONE BIT OF FLOOR IS A LONG WAY FROM AN INTACT ROMAN

villa," David told Dr. Pierson as they packed up their tools for the evening.

Pierson had decided to cover the floor again but mark it, placing stones around the edges of the hole so animals or wandering humans would not fall through the pocket of earth as David had.

"Even if I find only this mosaic, I will be happy," Pierson said with continued good cheer. "I knew I was right."

"Yes, you were." David clapped him on the back. Sophie had already headed for the house, her trim form a fine sight moving down the path toward the vicarage. "I have a suggestion. Let me send word to my friend El—the Duchess of Kilmorgan. She's an amazing photographer. If anyone can capture this floor before it's damaged by sun, wind, water, or curious antiquities seekers, it is she."

Pierson's brows went up. "Eleanor, the woman you wished to marry?"

David waved the objection away. "That was a long time ago. We're both older and far more sensible. Besides, she's madly in love with her husband."

Pierson looked at him in his penetrating way. "What about you?"

"Me?" David attempted a grin. "I do admire Hart and consider him a great friend, but I'm not in love with him, no."

"You know I meant his wife," Pierson said without humor.

David gazed at the arches of the ruined abbey in the distance, the evening made bleaker because Sophie had reached the vicarage and gone inside. He preferred to dance around truth because truth could be so exposing, embarrassing, and gut-wrenching, but he was ready to acknowledge things had changed in his life.

"I am no longer in love with Eleanor Ramsay." He could say

it with clarity, because it was true. "As I said, that foolishness was a long time ago. I am now *friends* with the Duchess of Kilmorgan. She truly is the best photographer in Britain, but no one will admit that because she's a woman. All smile about her dabbling, more fool they. If you want a good record of this find, invite her."

"What about Sophie?"

David growled in irritation. "Why are you asking me about all these ladies? What about Sophie? I imagine she will welcome the assistance. I'm obviously useless except by accident."

He touched the cheek that still smarted from landing on ancient decorative stone. His elbow, knee, and hip didn't feel sound either, and his new suit was much torn and grimy. Why he'd bothered with the damned thing, he had no idea.

Yes, he did know. He'd wanted Sophie to think him both well turned out and practical-minded. Circumstances had proved him neither.

"You are deuced obtuse sometimes, Fleming," Pierson surprised him by saying. "I will speak plainly so you will understand. Sophie is forming a tenderness for you, whether I approve or not. It would be awkward for her if the woman you once proposed to pushed her way in to our dig."

David listened in amazement. "What the devil are you talking about—a tenderness? Sophie wishes me at the bottom of the sea. She'd have left me in that hole, and good riddance, if I hadn't fortuitously landed on a bit of Roman tile. Besides, Eleanor would never push her way in. In spite of the way she rattles on, she is a perceptive woman. She'll give all credit to you and Sophie for the floor, snap her photographs, and go home. I suggested her because your books will be treasured forever if you include brilliant photographs to accompany your rather dry prose. But if you want blurred shots from, say, myself, then by all means, keep Eleanor far away."

David was surprised at his vehemence, and at Pierson's silence. He wished the world would find something else to talk about besides David's youthful passions. He had let Eleanor go in his heart some time ago—he would be happy when everyone else caught up.

"I see." Pierson watched him a while longer, reminding David without words that this man was far wiser than he liked to let on. He at last gave David a terse nod. "I suppose we can write to the duke."

"Or I could be terribly efficient and telegraph Eleanor this evening. Knowing her, she'll set off at once and arrive by morning."

Pierson shook his head. "You do like to rush about where angels fear to tread."

"Always have. But you want your floor recorded for posterity, don't you? Best to start immediately."

The appeal to his find clinched matters, as David knew it would. Pierson gave in with a sigh.

"Off you go. Send your wires. I'll break the news to Sophie."

He turned and shuffled toward the vicarage, the very picture of a worried guardian.

He worried for no reason, David thought irritably as he turned up the collar of his coat, settled his mud-smeared hat, and took the path to the village and its train station, which housed the telegraph office. Sophie didn't give a damn about David's past, nor would she feel any awkwardness about Eleanor. Why should she?

He was correct that Sophie would be very glad to see the back of David Fleming. He knew it in his bones.

SOPHIE WAS UP EARLY THE NEXT MORNING, WASHED AND dressed, her hair neat, her boots scrubbed free of yesterday's earth. She paced to the edge of the garden, pretending to take air after breakfast—so what if she timed the walk to coincide with the arrival of the Duchess of Kilmorgan?

Ever since Uncle had come in last evening announcing that David was striding to the village to telegraph the woman, Sophie hadn't been able to settle herself.

The duchess was one of the best-known hostesses in London. The ladies of the haut ton either adored Eleanor or reviled her, depending on their husbands' political stances. Laurie had commanded that the duchess be nowhere on Sophie's guest lists.

Therefore, Sophie did not know what to expect from her. She'd seen Eleanor at art openings and the like, which ladies from different factions attended, as long as they kept to their own sides of the room. The duchess was a red-haired woman who was very stylish though not a slave to fashion. She'd wafted about, unbothered by anyone's opinions, and Sophie had envied her effortless grace.

Sophie was not surprised David had fallen madly in love with Eleanor. She charmed all who came near her.

Today, this paragon would arrive at the stone vicarage in a tiny village in the middle of nowhere to photograph Uncle's mosaic. Not because she was a keen observer of archaeology or out of kindness for Uncle Lucas. She was coming because David asked her to.

David had been quite cheerful when he'd returned to the vicarage, missing tea, to Mrs. Corcoran's annoyance. He'd waved the duchess's return missive in triumph, his spirits high that she'd agreed to come.

Today. Now.

A plain black coach belonging to the stationmaster turned

down the lane and headed for the vicarage and Sophie in the garden.

Sophie had expected a duchess to turn up in an elegant landau emblazoned with the ducal coat of arms, eschewing the ordinary train to travel in elegance. But David had said she'd come by rail, chugging out of London at an ungodly hour.

"No hour is ungodly," Uncle had chided him gently, and David only grinned.

The coach slowed, the beefy man who doubled as a porter at the station pulling the horses to a halt. He climbed down ponderously, but before he could open the passenger's door, a lady's gloved hand reached through the open window and yanked at the handle.

"Ah," David's voice came behind Sophie. "There you are, old thing." He strode down the path, air wafting as he passed, and gallantly reached for the descending lady. "Good of you to rush to our aid."

A trim foot in a laced-up boot landed on the iron step, followed by a narrow gray tweed skirt that matched a gray jacket buttoned to the duchess's chin. A wide but plain hat covered a pompadour of red hair, no flowers or feathers or birds that liberally sprinkled women's hats these days in sight. The duchess had dressed practically for poking about muddy fields, it seemed. Sophie wasn't certain why the fact irritated her.

As soon as the duchess's feet touched the ground, she turned back to the carriage and tugged a case from it. "Don't call me *old thing*, and do be useful, David. There is much more in the carriage and another cart coming from the station."

She thrust the case into David's hands and turned a wide smile on Sophie. "How delightful to meet you, Miss Tierney. I believe I saw you at the Royal Academy presentation last year, but of course, I was instructed to snub you, as your husband and mine are on the opposite ends of the political spectrum. Yours wants Scotland firmly under England's thumb, and Hart wants all claymores raised until the Stone of Scone returns to Edinburgh. But that should not preclude us from being friends. We ladies have to stick together, no matter what our husbands get up to, do you not think?"

CHAPTER 9

The duchess laced her arm through Sophie's as she spoke, and turned her up the path to the vicarage. Sophie pressed her lips closed against all the questions she wanted to ask and let the duchess more or less march her to the house. Behind them, David threw himself into helping the coachman unload Eleanor's things, his voice cheerful.

Uncle Lucas appeared on the doorstep. He'd dressed in his clerical collar and one of his best black coats, though his next service wouldn't be until the morrow.

"Your Grace." He bowed awkwardly. "Welcome to this humblest of abodes. I hope we can make you comfortable, but I am skeptical about that, really."

Eleanor stepped inside and took in her surroundings with obvious pleasure. "Nonsense, I prefer small and cozy over large, damp, and draughty any day. Castles such as the one I grew up in are romantic to look at but not to live in, I assure you. And do please dispense with formality. I am Eleanor. If it offends your propriety to address a lady thus, Lady Eleanor will do, though I imagine we will all be shouting at each other by the end of the week without bothering with names."

Mrs. Corcoran had left her kitchen in time to hear the last of the speech. She curtseyed. "I'll take you to your chamber, Your Grace. It's a bit small but I've warmed it well."

"Palatial compared to mine," David said as he struggled in, breathless from his load of cases. "I'm in a closet under the rafters. How you fit a bed up there, Pierson, I have no idea."

"It was here when I arrived," Uncle answered without worry. "Are these the photographic apparatus? How exciting."

Eleanor made Mrs. Corcoran happy by going off with her, her effusions of gratitude floating back to them. Uncle hovered over the cases, and David straightened up, pushing his hair from his face. He winked at Sophie, and in spite of Sophie's nervousness, she wanted to laugh.

Somehow, the duchess and all her equipment was settled, and she shared a brief luncheon with them before they trooped out to look at the mosaic. Sophie had assumed the woman would want to rest the remainder of the day and perhaps be carried to the site on a litter with a host of servants by her side. Silly, yes, but Sophie hadn't known what to expect.

What she discovered was that Eleanor was a fairly normal human being, who'd grown up penniless, in spite of being an earl's daughter, and appeared at home in the misty countryside. At luncheon she'd steered the conversation to archaeology, getting Uncle to tell her not only about the villa, but other things he'd dug up in the past. By the time the meal was finished, Uncle was besotted, and Eleanor eager to see the mosaic.

The four walked out, each carrying a case of photographic equipment. The day was gray, but a luminous glow seemed to surround the field.

"A most excellent specimen," Eleanor proclaimed as she

gazed down at the tiled floor. "The artistry is remarkable, is it not? A piece from so far in the past, and yet we can touch it in the present." She let out a happy sigh. "Now then, it will be a challenge to photograph in this light. Miss Tierney, if you don't mind, I will need your help with reflectors and such. Dr. Pierson, you ought to also have an artist sketch this. Why not David? He draws like an angel."

"Do angels draw?" David asked in his lazy way. "I wouldn't think they'd have the time, what with all the harping and having to look after sinners like me."

"You know what I mean. If you do not have a sketch pad and pencils, procure some, please. The photos might not turn out, but a very good drawing will preserve this mosaic for all time. Like the *Description de l'Égypte* by Napoleon's savants."

David looked dismayed. "I'm not certain my draftsmanship is up to theirs."

"No matter. It will be good enough. Now, may I go down? Miss Tierney, will you accompany me?" Eleanor scrambled into the hole with only Uncle's hand to guide her.

Sophie wouldn't dream of remaining on solid ground while the duchess dropped into the dirty cave. She began to follow, then started when a pair of strong hands caught her around the waist.

She looked up into David's face, too close, his eyes briefly meeting hers. He lifted her, then set her gently down on the edge of the mosaic. Sophie caught Eleanor's glance and the hint of her smile before the duchess turned away.

"Mmm." Eleanor gazed about, careful not to step directly on the tiles. "Reflectors, definitely. We'll have to beam light here, and here." She pointed. "David will have to help. He *can* work hard, contrary to the indolent nature he displays."

"I do hear you, El," David said from above.

"It's rather foolish of him, this decadent man-about-town he insists upon portraying, when very few work longer hours or do more than Mr. Fleming. And then he gazes at one in astonishment when praised for his accomplishments."

"I'll be returning to London, I think." David's tone was pained. "Then you can talk me over to your heart's content while I sip brandy in my warm and comfortable club."

"Nonsense, I need you here to hold things." Eleanor dusted off her hands. "I will have to ponder how to arrange my gear, but for now, I believe a cup of tea for us all will be best."

The bulk of David's body blocked the light as he bent over the hole. "Do you mean we lugged all this out here only to lug it back again?"

"Of course not," Eleanor said, her blue eyes wide. "We can store it in Dr. Pierson's shed. But the light is too bad today, and shooting into this hole will be tricky. We might as well have a nourishing cup of tea while we make plans. Help us out, will you, gentlemen?"

Sophie could only admire how Eleanor mustered the troops. Within minutes, the equipment was stored, and they strolled back to the vicarage.

Eleanor, her arm firmly through Sophie's, slowed her steps, letting the gentlemen surge ahead. When David hesitated to wait for them, Eleanor waved him off. David's expression turned wary, but he walked on, catching up to Uncle Lucas who was bent on the warm vicarage and tea.

"Now then, my dear," Eleanor began. "I doubt we'll have much time to ourselves, so you must tell me everything immediately."

Sophie wet her lips, which the wind had dried. "Everything about what, Your Grace? I mean, Lady Eleanor."

Eleanor gave her a patient look. "You know exactly what I

mean. Your marriage, your divorce, why David is meddling in it, and what you think of him. I see the way you look at him, so it is obvious to me what is in your head, but I want to hear it from your lips. Are you in love with him?"

Sophie jerked to a halt. "In love?" she stammered. "How can I be? I barely know him."

"The heart does not always wait for such practical things. When I first met Hart Mackenzie, I told myself he was an arrogant, high-handed wretch who thought too much of himself and needed to be kicked squarely in the backside. I was right, of course, but at the same time, I fell hopelessly in love with him. Common sense told me to turn a cold shoulder, but my inconvenient emotions urged me to smile at him and kiss him silly at the first opportunity. Ah, my dear, I see your blush. You already have kissed David silly."

The duchess's very perceptive gaze made Sophie's face go hotter.

"Not deliberately," she managed.

"It was indeed deliberate, my dear. If you'd found David repugnant, you'd have punched him in the nose and marched away, demanding your uncle turn him out for the scoundrel he is. That means David kissed you, and you did not mind."

"No." Sophie had to face what was in herself. "I did not."

Eleanor's crooked smile warmed her. "Well then, we must retrieve you from this wretched marriage so you can kiss David with impunity."

Sophie gave a bitter laugh. "My husband is trying to push me from it quite eagerly."

"In a most inelegant and shameful way. Never mind. We shall see what happens."

She looked mysterious, and Sophie's misgivings rose. "David ... Mr. Fleming hinted there could be an annulment, but that is impossible. What do you know of it? I see by your face you know *something*."

"I do. But I do not wish to raise your hopes. Let me simply say that Mr. Fleming knows powerful people, my husband included in that number. They will work, and we shall await the outcome."

"Why should they?" Sophie ceased walking, facing the duchess as the wind tugged at hats and skirts. "Why should powerful men care about the bad marriage of the Earl of Devonport and his nobody wife?"

Eleanor regarded her calmly. "You are an intelligent young woman, I can see. Why do you suppose?"

Sophie did not believe her face could grow any more scalding. "You are saying David ... Mr. Fleming ... cares for me. I think you're wrong. I think he is trying to redeem himself—perform a good deed and be praised by his friends, or be forgiven for his past, or ... I don't know. He was very much in love with *you*." Sophie looked straight into the duchess's blue eyes. "Perhaps he is trying to gain your admiration."

"He is always attempting to gain my admiration," Eleanor said without concern. "And Hart's. That does not mean he cares nothing for you."

"He was in love with you," Sophie said, exasperated out of her politeness.

"Not at all." Eleanor's tone turned brisk. "David *liked* me very much—he still does, bless him—and he felt sorry for me. David lives very much in Hart's shadow—he usually prefers that, but it can't be easy. He took the opportunity once Hart's shadow moved to propose to me, but I knew full well we'd never suit. David knew that too once he worked through his wounded vanity. He is neither a slave to his emotions nor a fool."

Sophie listened in disquiet. Uncle Lucas had implied that

David had nearly wrecked his life for this woman, and she'd observed how easily Eleanor and David had fallen in with each other upon her arrival.

Because they had been friends for so long? Were they that comfortable with each other?

Sophie envied them this, even under her flare of jealousy. How lovely to have such a friendship. If the world were a different place, she could live forever with Uncle in the vicarage, friend David appearing for long stays, the three of them growing closer as the years passed.

But the world was not comforting. It preferred Sophie to either be married or widowed, to have no bodily desires, and to not dwell under the same roof as an unmarried gentleman, even with her uncle as a chaperone. Her bubble of coziness here would come to an end soon, never to be repeated.

Eleanor turned with Sophie and began walking again, in silence this time, sweeping her gaze over the landscape.

Sophie studied her curiously. "What about you, Lady Eleanor? You mentioned your husband's shadow—you must live constantly in it, as I do in my husband's. How do you manage?"

"Easily," Eleanor answered without rancor. "I side-step right back into the sunshine. Drives Hart spare." She smiled broadly, a woman confident in her own life and power.

Sophie had once thought she was as confident. Now she swam in a sea of confusion.

"You must be very happy," she said glumly.

Eleanor pulled her closer and patted her hand. "You must not give way, my dear. We will see that *you* are happy. I have determined this. I am so determined that Hart rolled his eyes at me and sent me away. Which means he agrees with me." Another pat as Eleanor gazed across the fields again. "What lovely country. I believe there are picturesque ruins of an abbey that I can photograph, are there not? I will have so many plates to develop I'll not come out of my darkroom for weeks." She squeezed Sophie's arm and smiled excitedly. "What a treat."

David watched Sophie as she held a mirror to beam a ray of sunlight onto the floor. She remained patient while Eleanor repositioned her camera a dozen times, none of the angles right, or so she claimed.

David hunkered on the other side of the mosaic with his mirror, he and Sophie trying to send the faint light onto the tiles. They'd cleared the hole and shored up its walls, but even so, it was tight quarters.

"You had to unearth the smallest Roman villa in creation," David called up to the hovering Dr. Pierson. "Instead of the lavish Golden House of Nero."

"I'm certain even bits of *that* found will be small," Pierson said without rancor. "It has been two thousand years, my friend. We cannot expect vast parlors for us to lounge in."

"I don't see why not. The Romans were fond of lounging. They ate dinner lying down."

"Must have been a messy business." Eleanor bent over her camera, covering her head with a black cloth to shut out what there was of the light. "I can't tuck into a cream cake at tea without dropping it all over my clothes."

David's imagination flashed to Sophie biting into the profiterole, cream sliding over her lips.

She must have thought about it at the same instant, because her eyes sought David's, and they shared a hot look.

He flinched at how much his heart turned over at her smile. When Sophie walked away once she was free, David would hurt, and hurt excessively. He knew it, but could he climb out of this hole and leave now, to get the pain over with?

No, of course not. He'd remain and be tortured by what he could not have. It was his way.

"Ah, there we are. Now, David, for the love of all that's holy, do not move. Oh, forgive me, Vicar."

"Not at all, my dear," Uncle Lucas said. He gazed eagerly into the opening, out of the light—Eleanor had already scolded him about casting shadows.

David tried to become a statue. Sophie, her arms a graceful curve as she held the mirror, did the same.

She'd make a beautiful sculpture, David thought. Like the Daphne of Bernini, or the glorious marble perfection of a Canova. It would of course be a nude statue, every curve of her delectably caught, her limbs displayed for all to see. But it would be a private thing, for the two of them ...

"*David,*" Eleanor said in exasperation. "Do pay attention."

David snapped his mind from its treacherous path. "I beg your pardon, old friend."

"And cease calling me *old*. No lady likes the adjective, even when she's ninety."

"I am devastated to upset you, my friend from the far-off days of my callow youth."

The light from Sophie's mirror wavered. David, who had not looked away from her for a moment, knew she was laughing.

Eleanor flung off the black cloth. "Well, I have done my best, but I see that I cann*ot* have the pair of you down here at the same time. You are conspiring to ruin my work."

Sophie's mirror shook harder, and David fell in love with her a little bit more.

"Good heavens," Pierson rumbled above, but he'd left the lip of the hole. "I wasn't expecting you so soon."

All three on the mosaic rose and peered over the edge in bewilderment. David thought they must look like moles poking out of their burrow to see the wide world.

A tall man with a thick brown beard, a brown suit in nearly the same shade, gaiters, and a shapeless hat walked toward Pierson, his arm outstretched. "Well met, Dr. Pierson."

"Indeed. Indeed." Pierson engulfed the man with his usual enthusiastic handshake and turned him to the three faces watching them. "My friends, this is Dr. Gaspar. Howard Gaspar. I took your advice to heart, Fleming, and decided to ask a professional archaeologist to help me with the site. I wrote to him while you were away."

"At your service." Dr. Gaspar bowed politely to the company.

His surname was Hungarian but he dressed, sounded, and behaved like an Englishman. Probably had never set foot in Hungary. He had brown eyes, brown hair, and sun-bronzed skin that blended with his rather shabby suit. *Drab,* David thought. Extraordinarily drab. Probably worked hard at it.

David knew bloody well he'd not have disparaged the man if Gaspar hadn't stared in a rude and intrigued way at Sophie. As Pierson assisted first Eleanor then Sophie to solid ground, Gaspar gazed at Sophie as though he'd been clouted between the eyes.

Exactly as David must have appeared when *he'd* first seen Sophie. Damn it all.

"May I present the Duchess of Kilmorgan," Pierson said grandly. "She's agreed to do the photography. And my niece, Miss Tierney."

Gaspar paid little attention to the fact that he was in the presence of a lofty duchess, because his interest was all for Sophie. David expected him to say something about envying Pierson for being surrounded by beauty, or exclaim that no great find could compare to the ladies—something smarmy and overblown.

Gaspar managed to stammer, "How do you do?" and then went silent.

Sophie took the hand he offered after he'd shaken Eleanor's and smiled at him. It was an admiring smile, a welcoming smile.

"How very nice to meet you, Dr. Gaspar. Uncle Lucas has spoken so highly of you."

She sounded happy to see him. David slipped as he climbed out, and ended up with mud all over his hands and knees.

Stifling curses, he made a show of comically wiping the earth away, but no one had noticed. Not Pierson, or Gaspar, or even Eleanor, blast her.

Most oblivious of all was Sophie. She continued to hold Gaspar's hand and smile into his face, and David's spirits went straight to hell.

CHAPTER 10

*T*hings did not improve over tea. Dr. Gaspar had recently returned from the Near East, where he'd been digging up Nineveh, and the ladies were full of eager questions.

Damn and blast that David had to admire intelligent women. Eleanor was the daughter of Britain's foremost botanist, and she'd done the photographs and plates for all his published works. Now she was reading her way through the Mackenzies's formidable library. David joked from time to time that she'd married Hart to get at his books, and Eleanor never corrected him.

Sophie's Uncle Lucas was not only a vicar but a Cambridge fellow, who, it was clear, had taught his niece many things about archaeology and ancient history. Instead of inquiring where on earth Nineveh lay—David had only the vaguest idea himself—she asked Dr. Gaspar if he'd seen Ashurbanipal's library and had the Babylonians left anything of it when they'd sacked the city?

Gaspar warmed under the ladies' interest and began to hold forth without arrogance. He told delightful anecdotes about how the local men and the donkeys had always gotten the better of him, which made the company, David excepted, laugh in merriment.

Dr. Gaspar wasn't much older than David, David decided, even if harsh climates had left lines on his skin. The beard made him look more elderly as well, though there wasn't a gray hair in it. He must have been at university around the same time as David—it turned out that Pierson had been one of Gaspar's tutors.

David had no memory of him. Either Gaspar had been finished by the time David arrived, or he'd existed in a world of reclusive scholars while David had sown his wild oats with Hart at his side. There had been times when David had barely remembered his own name, let alone those of his fellow undergraduates.

"Are you pleased to be home?" Sophie asked Gaspar when he paused for breath. "Or do you miss the excitement of the Arab lands?"

Gaspar considered the question. "There are benefits to England. Tea." He lifted his cup. "And a comfortable, dry home with a jolly fire, good food, and fine company." He raised the cup again. "But there is much to miss about the desert. Its weather suits me better than the damp air here. You would think we'd be isolated and know nothing of the wide world, but in fact, I learn news there almost quicker than in my lodgings in Cambridgeshire. Gossip abounds, and anyone who goes into town is bombarded when he returns to the dig. We learn of events not only in Britain—we have news from so many countries."

Eleanor gave him a sage look. "I believe you are itching to be off again, Dr. Gaspar."

"Perhaps. But when Dr. Pierson wrote me about this Roman villa, I had to come. I can coordinate the excavation here before I return to the Ottoman lands."

Everyone but David smiled, pleased with him.

"In that case, I'll run up to London," David said, trying to sound nonchalant. "Now that you have a much better expert at digging in the dirt, Pierson." He gave Gaspar what he hoped was a gracious nod.

"Nonsense," Pierson answered in surprise. "I can always use another man with a shovel."

"For which you can hire a villager. I have business to attend."

Sophie glanced at him, but said nothing. Whether she gave a damn if David came or went, he couldn't say.

On the other hand, Eleanor's glare held volumes. "Business you have other people looking into for you. Or do you mean you need to look into other people's business?"

Sophie quickly lifted her teacup, smothering her delicate cough.

"Very amusing, ol— I mean, *dear* friend," David said. "I have much to do, as always. I've rusticated here far too long."

"No, no, my good fellow," Pierson said. "You came here for sanctuary, and I believe you need to remain for a time."

True, both Fellows and Sinclair had counseled him to stay out of London as much as possible until his trial. Or, if he insisted on London, to remain home, under a voluntary house arrest.

Well, he couldn't be in a much more remote spot in England than Pierson's vicarage in Shropshire. David could walk outside whenever he wanted here, no locks or chains to keep him in, because there was nowhere to escape *to*.

"Perhaps not London," David said after a swallow of tea. "I might return to the old family farm."

"Oh, you are a farmer?" Gaspar asked with sudden interest. "Very like an archaeologist, is a farmer, except you dig to help living things and we dig to find dead things."

The room found his wit outstanding.

"Not much for farming, me," David said when they'd calmed themselves from the hilarity. "My pater left me an estate in Hertfordshire. Lovely country, though I'm apt to let the steward do as he pleases with the arable."

Gaspar's expression didn't change. "Quite a responsibility, a large landholding. I am not surprised you don't want to leave it for long."

Now David felt Sophie's eyes upon him, a hard stare as she sipped tea. Could he never please her?

"I don't mind rushing out to help Dr. Pierson with his hobby when he needs me," David said. "But we will be a bit crowded here. I should at least make way for a new guest."

"Not at all," Gaspar said quickly. "I am putting up in the village. And archaeology is not a hobby, my good sir. It is a science, revealing knowledge of the past—we learn many astonishing things we never understood even from the writings of the ancients. Pieces from a faraway age tell us much about day-to-day life of the ordinary person, as well as of kings."

He did not speak with rancor but as a learned man instructing a simpleton.

David clutched his teacup and bared his teeth in a grin. He who could hold a roomful of lords and ladies, princes and princesses, bishops and archbishops in the palm of his hand, was losing a battle against a vicar, an academic, and two beautiful women.

Before he could speak, Eleanor said, "Besides, I want to photograph the nearby abbey ruins, and you and Sophie need to show them to me."

"An excellent idea," Pierson said, far too earnestly. "We will all go. An outing away from the dig will do me good, and I can tell Dr. Gaspar all about it as we walk. The abbey at Weston is lovely, the cloisters amazingly well preserved—Cromwell's men fortunately missed it when they were kicking over ancient churches."

And so, David, instead of being able to flee to the solitude of his London flat or the green fields of Moreland Park in Hertfordshire, found himself roused from sleep at dawn the next morning by Eleanor's brisk knock.

"Come along, David," she said through the closed door. "We are about to set off. We're waiting for you, so do get up. At once, please, there's a good fellow."

SOPHIE KNEW DAVID HAD NO WISH TO ACCOMPANY THEM TO the abbey ruins, and only Eleanor's prodding had him on the path a half hour after she woke him.

He dressed in the tweeds he'd brought back from his London sojourn, cleaned and pressed by Mrs. Corcoran, but he'd quickly ruin the suit in the damp. He looked like a dandy trying to fit into the country and failing miserably.

Dr. Gaspar, in plain brown flannel and thick-soled boots, was prepared to be grimy by the end of the day. A professional archaeologist, Sophie mused as she studied him. She would meet more of them as she followed Uncle about the world.

David trudged along, burdened with Eleanor's tripod, which he balanced over his shoulder, as well as two of her cases. Sophie carried a satchel with sandwiches Mrs. Corcoran had pressed on her, knowing Uncle often forgot to eat. She'd also brought pencil and paper—while Eleanor photographed, Sophie might do a sketch of the ruins. She didn't consider her drawing skill up to much, but she enjoyed it.

"May I carry that for you?" Dr. Gaspar, at her side, reached for the satchel.

Sophie jumped. "No, no," she said breathlessly. "You are kind, but it isn't heavy."

Dr. Gaspar looked embarrassed. "Oh. I beg your pardon. I did not mean to insult ..."

Sophie smiled at him. "Never mind. You startled me, is all. I would be grateful for your help."

Dr. Gaspar eagerly closed his fingers around the handle. The satchel was indeed light, and he overbalanced, expecting a greater weight. He danced a few steps and then righted himself, laughing a little.

Poor man. Like many of Uncle's acquaintance, Dr. Gaspar wasn't certain how to behave in company. She would have to put him at his ease.

She caught David's eye on her, the man scowling like a thunderstorm. Upset Dr. Gaspar hadn't offered to help *him*? Or upset at Sophie for some reason? Drat the man—he confused her so.

"Weston Abbey was founded in the eleventh century," Uncle held forth as they walked. "The Augustinians built an enormous cloister and church, which was of course sacked by Henry the Eighth when he had his little disagreement with the Pope. It was one of the wealthiest, I have heard, and the king and his men took everything, leaving it to ruin. Wonderful place for a picnic."

The abbey, which decorated the distant views from the vicarage, grew more imposing as they approached it. The stark ribs of the fallen church on the hill never failed to move Sophie— forlorn, forgotten beauty, a once proud place now silent and deserted. The golden stone against blue sky held stark and yet warm beauty. She could imagine the monks of centuries past toiling in the fields before returning to the golden-bricked cloisters for prayer and rest.

"They had a large scriptorium, Uncle tells me," Sophie said to Dr. Gaspar as they trundled up the hill. "Records show they copied many books over the four hundred years they were here. All lost now."

Dr. Gaspar halted, aghast at her words. "Terrible. What a waste."

Sophie nodded. "Sad when people value books so little. They stripped the abbey of its riches and discarded what they considered useless."

"Men tend to be dazzled by a book's gold bindings and not the words inside," Eleanor agreed. "If those soldiers could even read them. Most were in Latin, I imagine. Or Greek."

"'Look on my works, ye mighty, and despair!'" David burst out.

Dr. Gaspar, Uncle, and Eleanor stared at him as though he'd lost his mind. David, flushing, quieted. "It's Shelley. *Ozymandias*. I thought it fitting."

Sophie wanted to laugh. His look was so contrite, Dr. Gaspar's confused, that their present comedy outweighed the sad loss of the past.

"We're almost there," Sophie declared. "Our favorite place is just around the corner."

They soon lowered their burdens, David making a show of rubbing his back. Sophie spread blankets they'd brought and retrieved the satchel from Dr. Gaspar, unpacking it. Mrs. Corcoran has insisted on flasks of tea and porcelain cups from which to sip it.

Eleanor had the gentlemen setting up equipment for her, trying various angles to catch the best light. Sophie, once she'd finished laying out the food and drink left them to it and wandered away to the cloisters.

She'd loved this place on her visits to Uncle as a child. He hadn't objected to her exploring at will, asking him question after question. She'd learned so much more from Uncle Lucas about history and religion, the past and present, than from any book or lecture at her girls' seminary.

A large part of the cloister walls remained standing, arches that lined a courtyard rising gracefully. The abbey had been built in the Romanesque style, before the Gothic mania of the later medieval times, and had more rounded arches, plainer walls, a simplicity that touched her.

Beyond the walls, green hills stretched toward a river valley that marked the Welsh border.

"Amazingly peaceful," said a voice at her shoulder.

Sophie somehow had known he'd come, that he'd been there, admiring the beauty of the landscape with her.

"I loved it as a girl." Sophie rested her hand on an arch. "I pretended it was my castle, put here for me and Uncle. No one else could come."

"Then I'm intruding." David made no move to leave, relaxing against the bricks beside him.

"Of course not. You're a guest."

David frowned. "Don't sound so damned formal. A princess condescending to allow a peasant to bask in her company for a few moments."

"At a monastery? I'd be a nun, not a princess."

"You wouldn't be here at all. Except as a lady bountiful bestowing largess on the men who slaved away here day after day, copying books and brewing beer." He trailed off to a mutter. "As you do with Gaspar."

Sophie stared at him. "I beg your pardon? I am being polite, hardly bestowing largess. You, on the other hand, are appallingly rude to him. What the devil is the matter with you?"

"Rude?" David blinked. "When have I been rude? I thought I was being disgustingly unctuous."

"Rubbing his nose in the fact that you are a landed gentleman with a vast estate, when he can barely pay for a meal. Dr. Gaspar's father and mother ailed for a long time, eating up any money they had, leaving him destitute when they finally passed on. Uncle had to help him find work with a professor leaving for Constantinople. Dr. Gaspar has a brilliant mind, but he's paid only in room and board—a gentleman doesn't work for wages, does he? The sponsors of the digs have no intention of keeping him in luxury."

David's expression went stiff. "I hadn't realized that."

"And calling archaeology a hobby. How could you?" Sophie warmed to the topic. "You know how Uncle feels about his digs. As though you are not a dilettante in your ridiculous suit ..." She waved her hands at it.

David glanced down in surprise. "What is wrong with my suit? Shall I scramble about looking for Roman villas in evening dress?"

"Of course not. Don't be silly."

"My usual clothes are meant for clubs and meetings with other indolent gentlemen. I thought I'd purchase things I could ruin."

A Bond Street tailor had made his suit and made it well, Sophie recognized. Even Laurie, who spent money in great spews, would have taken good care of clothes like that.

"Whose approval do you seek?" Sophie asked, unable to halt her tongue. "Uncle's? Or Lady Eleanor's?"

David gave her an odd look. He began to answer, then checked himself. "Why should I seek their approval?"

Not what he'd meant to say. The question lacked conviction.

Sophie cast about for biting answers, but all she could manage was a lofty, "I am certain I have no idea."

David turned and folded his arms as he gazed out over the

fields below. After a time, his face smoothed, lines of anger vanishing.

"I could stay here forever," he said softly.

"But we can't." Sophie heard the regret in her voice. "The world marches on, and we must march with it."

"*Why* should we? The world has done its best to hound us until we retreated from it."

"Because I must await my fate, and you, I believe, must attend a trial to clear yourself of attempted murder."

"Ah, yes, mustn't forget Griffin." David stared at the distant hills without changing expression.

"You don't seem worried."

"Griffin has been determined to pot me one for years. Ever since I destroyed one of his proposals to increase a man's control over all monies his wife possesses, even those left to her in carefully worded trusts for her lifetime. He wanted to get his hands on the part of his wife's fortune he can't touch, is all. I remember being quite blatant in my ridicule. He's never forgiven me."

Sophie felt herself soften. "You spoke up for the ladies, did you?"

"I always do. The laws that keep them bound to tyrannical men are ridiculous and should have been done away with long ago. You are in the delicate position you find yourself because of those stupid laws, created to make women property so they'd be easier to control."

His face had flushed, his anger high. Sophie softened even more.

"I was also a giddy young woman who fell in love with a handsome man. What a fool I was to do that."

David took a minute step closer to her. "I don't think you fell in love, not really. You were charmed, is all. Lackwit Laurie is, I suppose, good-looking and can make himself agreeable." He gave her a wavering smile. "As I am not handsome and never agree-able, you have no need to worry about that in my case."

Sophie's heart beat faster. "You do yourself a wrong. I find you quite handsome."

His gray-blue eyes flicked to her, something in them she couldn't read. "I noticed you left off *agreeable*."

"I did."

"I love when you smile." David reached for her, cupping her face. "It's like the warmest sunshine."

Sophie strove for another quip, but thoughts deserted her as he touched her cheek, soft glove over a strong hand.

The memory of his kiss before he'd stormed away to London hadn't left her. It still seared on her lips, the tingle as fresh as though he'd kissed her a moment ago.

Sophie's body felt like water, her need to flow to him strong. As much as she'd been beguiled by her husband, she'd never felt for Laurie this attraction, the desire to touch and be touched by him.

The difference between a naive girl and a wiser woman, perhaps.

Or perhaps it was simply David—his haunted eyes, the lines around his mouth that deepened with his smile. His amazing strength, apparent in every move, the athletic hardness of a body he hid under well-made suits.

The way he looked at Sophie, truly *looked* at her, as though she was a person, not a female in attractive clothes meant to impress her husband's cronies. David listened to her when she spoke, argued with her or agreed with her, as though her opinion on a subject mattered.

Wind blew through the broken arches of the cloister, stirring Sophie's hair. It strengthened, taking David's cap. The tweed hat sailed down the hill and through the grass like a strange, flat bird.

"Damn and blast," David growled, and Sophie laughed.

He was off, chasing it. Sophie caught up her skirts and ran after him, David trying to pounce on the wayward headgear. The wind caught it again, snatching it from David's hands.

Sophie hurried down the hill, picking her way through the slippery grass, warmed by the sun. David missed again, but Sophie managed to stop the hat as it tumbled away by stepping on it.

She reached down and lifted the cap, gazing ruefully at her muddy boot print in the middle of the fabric. "Oh dear. I will order another one for you. Or you can wear one of Uncle's, though they are rather battered—"

David snatched the cap from her and threw it to the ground. "I don't care about the be-damned hat."

They stood on the steep side of the hill, the ruins looming above them. Easy to fall the short way to the grass touched with spring green, David's arms cushioning her.

They landed together, sprawled against the hill, David turning Sophie to him to cover her mouth in a burning kiss.

CHAPTER 11

Time slowed to a trickle as David kissed Sophie, an amazing, beautiful woman. Her mouth softened to his, she kissing him in return as she brushed his hair back with shaking fingers.

Grass tickled his leg, and the wind was sharp, but David ignored all but Sophie beneath him. Her breath touched his cheek, mouth caressing, teeth gently scraping his lip.

David eased the kiss to a close and took in her green eyes shining in the gray light, her face that haunted his dreams.

He touched her mouth, red and warm. "The beauty of you," he whispered. "It tore at me the moment I saw you."

"That sounds frightening." Sophie's smile was faint. "I don't want to hurt you."

"Too late for that. Being with you hurts me, and being without you is even worse."

The smile vanished. "I don't like being without you, either."

David stopped, his body going cold then hot. "Dear God, don't give me hope. Don't let me."

"I can't help it." Sophie's eyes were sad. "It is the truth."

David's breath choked him. He longed to push her back into the hill and let them seek peace in each other, no matter that her uncle and Eleanor and the irritating Gaspar lurked above, probably looking for them by now.

He wanted Sophie with intensity, wanted to peel her sensible clothes from her and lick her body, to gaze at every astonishing inch of her, to touch her. He pictured her ripping the suit she so disliked from him, and then exploring, stroking, the two of them bringing each other to life.

A sparkle in her eyes told him she wanted it too.

David slid on top of her, and she wrapped him in eager arms. They met in another kiss, this one frenzied, their veneer of politeness falling away. They were man and woman, needing, yearning, and on David's part, loving.

Sophie was a part of him he hadn't realized wasn't there. Her simply being in the world completed him.

She sought his mouth, and David let her in, needing her heady taste, the spice that was Sophie. Her lips were softness itself, her tongue brushing against his as the kiss turned harder.

David slid his hand between them, wishing they weren't wearing so many damned clothes. He cupped her breast, moving his thumb across her nipple, which tightened even through her corset.

Sophie made a noise of desire. She slid her firm hand to the back of his neck, tugging him closer.

Her kisses, full of passion, weren't practiced. Her stupid husband hadn't taught her, David realized, had ignored her needs. Sophie would never say so, but her inexperienced caresses told David more than words. She was a woman of fire, but that fire had never been allowed to flare.

David caressed her breast, slowly, not wanting to scare her

away. She looked up at him in languor, no fear at all. She wanted, she needed. She welcomed.

Their mouths met again, softly at first, then with more fervor. David nibbled her lip, his body on fire.

He rapidly considered places they could go, out of the wind and damp, to be alone, finish this. His mind fixed on nothing, wanting to be in the here and now, with Sophie.

Her mouth tasted like the finest wine and the deepest need. When she twined her foot around his leg, the warmth of her skirts enveloping him, he thought he'd die.

Shouts sounded above them, and David heard his name. Sophie gasped, their mouths clashing as she fought to sit up.

David quickly rolled from her and to his feet, reaching for Sophie to help her stand. He brushed at her clothes covered with grass, and felt her hands on him doing the same. They started to laugh, stifling it as they frantically batted away grass and mud.

Eleanor appeared over the crest of the hill. "Ah, there you are, my dears."

Sophie bent and retrieved David's now ruined and flattened cap. "David's hat blew away," she said quickly. "We were chasing it."

Eleanor only gazed at them, knowing damn well what they'd been doing hidden away from the others.

"I agree," she said in a loud voice. "The view is especially fetching. But now it's time for luncheon."

David held out a hand to assist Sophie up the hill. She touched his fingers as she ran lightly past him, Eleanor watching them come, wisdom in her eyes.

———

SOPHIE WAS NEVER SURE HOW SHE MANAGED THE NEXT DAYS.

David was always near, and she could barely breathe around him.

He'd touched something in her, sparking it to life. She'd never felt anything like it before, and realized now that she'd never loved Laurie. As David had so perceptively observed, she'd been only attracted to Laurie, as he could make himself agreeable when he wished.

She understood that Laurie had flattered her and been at his most gentlemanly around her so she'd marry him. Once he'd run through her money and it was clear she hadn't conceived his child, he'd been finished with her. Sophie might have been any woman, of any name, and it wouldn't have mattered. Laurie had no interest in her for herself.

David did. Sophie told herself to be careful, that she'd been cruelly deceived by Laurie, but this didn't feel the same.

David had no reason to woo her. She was legally still married, and she had no more dowry, no family connections, and no popularity that would help him. He had an estate, wealth, many friends, and seemed unconcerned about his bachelor state. He could have any mistress he wanted, and had apparently taken famous ones in the past.

What he saw in Sophie Tierney, a nonentity with a scandal in her life, she had no idea. But when David smiled at her, his eyes held need and warmth, caring.

Being with you hurts me, and being without you is even worse.

Sophie knew exactly what he meant. She held the words to her heart, and tried not to give herself away every time the two of them passed each other in the vicarage's narrow corridors.

On Sunday, they attended the village church. Uncle had convinced Sophie to play the organ, Mrs. Plimpton happy to stay at home and nurse her aching bones. The church, built in an age where even the smallest parishes sported grandiose Gothic structures, had an organ loft, so Sophie could perch there and not have to enter with the congregation.

Uncle spoke about Moses today, focusing on the story of the baby Moses being rescued from the reeds. He then compared Moses being chosen to lead the Isrealites to freedom to Jesus being born to redeem sinners, one foreshadowing the other. Two helpless children had become saviors.

Uncle then went on to talk about how archaeologists and historians argued whether the pharaoh in Exodus was Ahmose the First or Ramses the Great, and perhaps if there were enough excavations, they would find out for certain. Digging up the past, Uncle concluded, was much like human beings sifting through their own pasts to reveal their sins, confess them, and ask forgiveness.

The last had been tacked on, as though Uncle realized his congregation was nodding off over the history of Ramses. Sophie pumped the organ and plodded through the next hymn, while Uncle shook himself and returned to the rest of the service.

David glanced up from where he sat with Eleanor and Dr. Gaspar, and shot her a quick grin. Arrow to her heart.

Once they reached home, Mrs. Corcoran, after she'd removed her Sunday hat, handed David a small envelope.

"You've a telegraph message, Mr. Fleming. Village boy gave it to me as I was walking back."

David neatly slit the envelope with a pocket knife and slid out the paper inside. He read the brief missive then folded it, his eyes dark.

"I must return to London." His voice was easy but held a note that stirred Sophie's worry. "Is there a train up, Mrs. Corcoran?"

Mrs. Corcoran shook her head. "There's no train from our station 'til morning, very early. But the butcher's son is driving into Shrewsbury to be at the market tomorrow, and there's a mail train from there at four this afternoon."

"You are a walking Bradshaw, good lady," David said, impressed.

"I've lived here all my life," Mrs. Corcoran answered. "Stands to reason I know the trains. Not that there's many out our way, so I've come to know the Shrewsbury timetables as well."

"Excellent. I shall seek this butcher's son and beg him to take me in his cart."

Sophie did not like how heavy her heart grew as she listened to this exchange. She could say nothing, only swallow the lump in her throat.

Uncle Lucas gave David a surprised look. "Why the hurry to be off? Are they arresting you at last?"

Dr. Gaspar started, and even Eleanor looked concerned.

"No, indeed," David said quickly. "It's business that won't wait. I'll return as soon as I'm able."

"Not until you've had luncheon, certainly." Uncle led the way to the dining room as though brooking no argument.

Sophie tried to corner David as they went in, but he eluded her, slipping past Dr. Gaspar to escort Eleanor and seat her with aplomb.

Had the telegram to do with Sophie's divorce? She'd asked him to leave it alone, but she didn't believe for a moment he would. David was a whirlwind, Sophie had come to understand, and when he fixed on a problem, he'd sweep it up and pound on it until that problem surrendered in defeat.

"I believe I will accompany you, Mr. Fleming," Eleanor announced as Mrs. Corcoran brought in the meal—a cold one, as she did no cooking on Sundays. "I have taken many photographs, and I want to develop them in my darkroom at home."

Dr. Gaspar gazed at her in alarm. "Gracious, dear lady, you

cannot ride all the way to Shrewsbury in a butcher's cart. You are a duchess."

Eleanor sent him a pitying smile. "Well, I am not about to tramp to Shrewsbury with my photographic plates strapped to my back. Do not worry, Dr. Gaspar, I am not delicate porcelain. And I am certain David will give me the best seat on the cart."

"Of course." David winked at Sophie.

Sophie ate her cold beef without answering.

Eleanor shot Sophie what she supposed was meant to be a reassuring look. Sophie did feel a little better—Eleanor had decided to travel back so that she could keep an eye on David, Sophie surmised. Developing the photographs was an excuse.

After luncheon, David disappeared to his chamber at the top of the house, descending with his small valise. Eleanor had several large cases, which David and Dr. Gaspar gallantly loaded onto the cart for her. The butcher's boy, a placid youth, assisted, seemingly unbothered by his detour.

David turned to Sophie once the cases were safely stowed. "*Au revoir*, my lady." He gave her a sweeping bow, narrowly missing hitting his head on the cart's large rear wheel.

"I will take good care of him, dear." Eleanor caught Sophie's hand and kissed her cheek. "He needs looking after."

Sophie had been thinking things over since the day at the ruined abbey, and she'd come to a few conclusions. "Eleanor," she said, drawing the lady a few steps aside. "May I ask you to help me do something?"

She told Eleanor what she had in mind in a few short sentences, and Eleanor listened in delight.

"Well, of course." Eleanor sent her a broad smile, and then one to David, who looked suddenly suspicious. "Leave it to me. Wait for my message."

"Thank you."

Sophie squeezed Eleanor's hands, who returned the squeeze. Eleanor accepted Dr. Gaspar's assistance into the cart, David climbed up after her, and Uncle stood back and waved.

David tipped his hat to Sophie as the butcher's boy started the cart with a jerk, and they rolled away. His look held both curiosity and misgivings, but Sophie trusted that Eleanor wouldn't breathe a word.

DAVID SLEPT AT HIS LONDON FLAT THAT NIGHT, EVERY moment agony as he alternately missed Sophie and dreamed erotic dreams of her. In the morning he took time to bathe and make himself presentable before he turned up at a horribly early hour at Essex Court in Middle Temple to meet Sinclair, Lackwit Laurie, and a barrage of solicitors.

He had not been able to pry out of Eleanor what she and Sophie had been whispering about before he'd rolled away from the vicarage. Eleanor had only given him one of her serene gazes and spoke determinedly of other things. He was not certain whether to be worried or amused. Worried—he should most definitely be worried.

David reflected, as he reached Essex Court, that he'd grown so used to Pierson dragging him up at dawn that he entered the meeting at Sinclair's chambers relatively refreshed and wide awake.

On the other hand, Laurie, the Earl of Devonport, looked as though he'd been dragged from the warmth of sleep, poured into a suit, and dropped on Sinclair's doorstep. His eyes were bloodshot, his face flushed, his hands trembling with dissipation. David did not like to think that for most of his life, he had appeared the same.

"Fleming," Laurie said with a sneer as they all took chairs. "I am glad you've condescended to join us. We can put an end to this nonsense."

David crossed his elegantly booted feet. "Indeed. I look forward to you vanishing from Miss Tierney's life."

Laurie's sneer grew more pronounced. "So you can have her yourself, you libertine."

"You mistake me. I am acting as her friend, attempting to free her from a terrible situation. What she does after that is entirely up to her."

"Your idea of annulment has failed, damn you." Laurie clutched the arms of his chair, but his eyes gleamed in triumph. "As I am here to reveal."

Sinclair, who could be both silent and heavily present at the same time, adjusted his cuffs. Laurie's two solicitors fussed with papers, pretending to ignore their client's boorishness.

"Why are you so adamant about divorce?" David asked, as though merely curious. "Annulment will free you to re-marry without fuss. Divorce complicates matters."

"Because there are no grounds for annulment." Laurie nearly shouted the words. "As I told you before. I had no choice."

"Ah, so better that it is Sophie's fault than yours." David's voice went hard. "I warned you, Lackwit. You ought to have taken my advice."

"I did. I let myself be tested for impotence." Laurie flushed, as though too delicate for such matters. "A rather humiliating ordeal, but I am happy to report that I passed with flying colors."

"Poor man. The ladies pleased you, did they?"

"They did." Laurie smiled, his eyes sparkling.

Sinclair cleared his throat, a dry but powerful sound. "Perhaps, your lordship, you will let me share the testimony of the ladies in question?"

Laurie's flush deepened. "Why not? Then Fleming will leave me alone. That is, after I sue him for poking his fingers into my private business."

"That sounds disgusting." David sat back, resting his hands easily on the arms of his chair. "I wouldn't put my fingers anywhere near your private business. Carry on, McBride. Let us hear the worst."

Sinclair cleared his throat again. He was very good at it.

"I need not read the entire statement of either lady present at the examination. The gist from Mrs. Lane and Mrs. Whitaker is that at no time during the procedure did Lord Devonport show any physical response to them. They vow that he remained flaccid the entire hour." Sinclair dropped the paper, his cheekbones tinged red. "No matter how much or how often they tried."

Laurie gaped in astonishment. Not a pretty sight—he was developing jowls. Some men retained handsomeness for life, but Laurie wouldn't be one of them.

Laurie gripped the arms of his chair until his knuckles were white. "That is a damned lie. You're in *his* pay—of course you'd claim that." He glared at David then snarled at his solicitors. "Speak up. Read the statements. Do what I pay you for."

One of the solicitors raised his head, his expression strained. "We have the same testimony, my lord." He held up a sheaf of papers.

Laurie sprang to his feet. "But it's a bloody falsehood. My cock stood like a soldier at attention from the moment they started on me. More than that. I had Mrs. Lane, had her several times right there on the floor. She was most willing, squealed quite fetchingly. Then I went to my mistress and had *her* several times that night. Not only am I *not* impotent, gentlemen, I am most healthily robust."

David rose in one smooth motion and faced the triumphant

Earl of Devonport, while the solicitors looked away, painfully embarrassed. Sinclair sat like a stone, but his eyes glittered with resolve.

"I am glad you said that," David stated to Laurie in a quiet voice. "It allows you a choice. You can either agree with this testimony as it stands and proceed with an annulment, or I and Mr. McBride can be witnesses for Sophie that you are an adulterer many times over, and she needs a divorce from *you*."

Laurie's chin came up. "I'll not let you bully me into telling lies. This isn't school anymore, Devilish David. The divorce proceedings I began will go forward. Count on that."

"No, they won't." David had hoped he'd taste triumph at this moment, but only revulsion filled his mouth. "You have no more witnesses. The gentlemen you bribed to make false statements against Miss Tierney have withdrawn them. They admitted they were liars and that you paid and coerced them to claim they'd had relations with your wife. They never did, and they have signed sworn statements saying the same. Lady Devonport is spotless and innocent, and you will proclaim that to the world, Lackwit. What you have done to her, your duplicitous scheme to ruin your own wife in a loathsome fashion, is all over London, and I doubt that after this, any house will receive you."

CHAPTER 12

*L*aurie's mouth had dropped open once more, and his face was mottled red and white.

"You'd ruin me?" he demanded of David. "You heard this, did you not, gentlemen?" He appealed to his solicitors. "Those women are damned liars—likely in Fleming's pay. You'd take the word of courtesans over that of a gentleman?"

By the solicitors' expressions, they would.

Sinclair, at David's behest, had made certain the solicitors would take the depositions Mrs. Whitaker and her protégé, Mrs. Lane, gave as legal testimony. The ladies had played their parts well, swearing up and down that Laurie was as impotent as a castrated bullock. David would send Mrs. Lane a lavish gift for putting up with Laurie's despicable attentions, and Mrs. Whitaker one for orchestrating their part of the scheme.

"I want to be tested again," Laurie snarled. "With ladies of *my* choosing."

"Do," David said. He knew plenty of courtesans, as did Mrs. Whitaker, who would make certain whoever Laurie chose would also claim him impotent.

Laurie recoiled. "Kilmorgan is behind this, I know it. He wants to impugn my character, to ruin me."

"The Duke of Kilmorgan had nothing to do with any of this," David said. He spoke the truth. Mrs. Whitaker, who had assisted David and Hart so much in the past, had done the favor because Eleanor asked her, not Hart. Mrs. Whitaker had much respect for El.

David looked into Laurie's eyes to read fear there. Laurie was losing ground, and he knew it.

"You've impugned your own character, ruined yourself," David said quietly. "The scandal-loving newspapers are already printing your perfidy now. I'd leave for the Continent soon, Limp-Prick. *After* you annul your marriage with Miss Tierney."

Laurie scowled at David, the petulant boy he'd once been shining through. He glanced at the solicitors and Sinclair, but those gentlemen sat silently, offering no help.

David lifted a pen from Sinclair's desk and shoved it at Laurie. "Mr. McBride has drawn up everything you need to begin proceedings for an annulment. Sign it."

"How dare you?" Laurie blustered. "You can't threaten me. This is a farce, and you a bloody scoundrel. You are Hart's arse-licking toady—what is his game? You fu—"

Laurie choked off the word as David caught the lapel of his coat, pressing the tip of the pen hard to Laurie's cheek. "How dare *you* make Miss Tierney's life a living hell? What you owe her you can never, ever repay. Now sign the bloody papers or this pen goes down your throat."

Laurie drew a breath to argue, but what he saw in David's eyes defeated him. He'd always been a coward, full of bravado and bullying, wilting whenever challenged in truth.

"Damn you." Laurie jerked himself from David's grip. "Damn you all."

He snatched the pen from David's hand and thrust it into the inkwell Sinclair held out to him.

"I'll ruin *you*, Fleming," he vowed. "I'll smear so much dirt on you, you'll never be able to stand for Parliament again."

"An empty threat," David said, his easy drawl emerging. "I'm a bit tired of it all, as a matter of fact. I plan to return home, make a go at farming."

Laurie glared fury at him. But he turned to the desk, and with a few strokes of the pen, started Sophie on her path to freedom.

SOPHIE HAD NEVER BEEN TO HERTFORDSHIRE, IN SPITE OF the county lying so near London. She knew of Hatfield, where Good Queen Bess had grown up, but she'd never traveled to look at that queen's historic house. Being the countess hadn't allowed her much time for herself.

David Fleming's estate lay in the north of the county, near its border with Bedfordshire. The train took Sophie and Uncle Lucas to the village of Clopdon—from there the stationmaster directed them two miles north to the house called Moreland Park.

As it was a fine day, and they had brought only one valise with their combined belongings, Uncle Lucas suggested they walk.

None at the station had questioned their intent to visit Moreland Park. The gardens were open for viewing, provided one paid a shilling to the gatekeeper, and on a certain day each month, the house could be toured as well.

The home itself hailed from the eighteenth century, built in the French style, kept well by the current landlord, if he rarely visited it. Mr. Fleming's father had purchased it about forty years ago when the line of the family who'd originally owned it died out. The Flemings, senior and junior, had spent much to restore and modernize the estate.

So had said the stationmaster, who regarded the house and grounds with much pride. The master wasn't a bad sort, he said, even if he preferred Town living to country.

"Glorious." Uncle Lucas gazed about in admiration as they trudged through a side gate from the lane to a vast front garden. "I had no idea David lived in such splendor."

A park with straight walks through greenery spread before them, spring bulb flowers emerging in symmetrical beds. Daffodils, tulips, and irises brushed bright yellow, orange, red, and purple through the green. The walks were pressed clay, stripes of burnt orange leading through the flowering splendor.

The house, in the style of a French chateau, was long and low, with three stories in its center wing, the top floor studded with dormer windows in a mansard roof. Two single-story wings flanked the main one, and a shallow flight of steps rose to a front terrace and a double-door entry.

Though the house was formal, Sophie found it inviting. Its soft golden stone shone in the afternoon sunshine, and French windows lined the ground floor. The entire scene suggested ladies and gentlemen moving casually about, strolling onto the terrace to enjoy a view of the garden, or back inside to warmth and a cup of hot tea.

"Have you never visited?" Sophie asked as she and Uncle Lucas made their leisurely way through the garden.

"Never had call to. I'm so pleased he's invited us now."

Sophie halted. Uncle walked onward for several yards before he realized she'd stopped, and glanced back in surprise.

"I did not realize you thought Mr. Fleming had invited us," Sophie said awkwardly. "He did not."

"No?" Uncle Lucas gazed across the garden as though expecting David to pop up from behind a box hedge and explain. "Then why have we come?"

Sophie's face went hot. "Lady Eleanor arranged it. I asked her to."

Uncle frowned in perplexity. "I am not certain I understand. Why not simply ask David to show you his house? It is open every third Thursday to the world, anyway."

"Because ..." Sophie was no longer certain, and she fumbled for an explanation. "He might have said no, and I wanted ... I wanted to see where he comes from. Learn more about him."

Uncle studied her, understanding in his eyes. "My dear, the man you see with us in Shropshire *is* Mr. Fleming. He does not change when he moves from place to place. I admit that some people do, but David has never been duplicitous. At least, not to his friends."

Sophie drew a breath, enjoying the clean air scented with flowers. "I am pleased to hear it, but ... I suppose I wish to understand him. He is a puzzling man."

"True, but we did not have to change trains three times and ride halfway across England so you can understand him. But, as we are here, we might as well make the best of it. Come along." He lifted the valise, which he had rested on the path while he spoke, and trudged toward the front door.

Sophie fell into step with him and studied the house as they approached it. "It is not where I imagined he'd live."

"His father purchased the estate." Uncle Lucas spoke breathily as they walked. "He was even more decadent than David—David learned his feigned lazy manner from him. David's father bought it for David's mother, but she died when David was quite young. His father then began to live a most extravagant and lavish lifestyle, collecting expensive artworks and hosting gatherings that became famous, if not infamous. Some said, uncharitably, that he celebrated his wife's death, but from what David has told me, the man was grieving. Trying to run away from his pain. He died falling from a racehorse in a steeplechase, leaving David alone as a very young man and quite rich."

Sophie's steps slowed as she listened. David must have grown up watching his father cover his deep feelings with self-indulgence and dissipation. This explained some of David's sardonic manner, the pain that lingered in his eyes. His father must not have known what to do with a small boy except teach him to be as extravagant as he was.

Uncle Lucas had already mounted the steps to the front door, and Sophie hurried to catch up.

"Perhaps we should not," she said quickly. "We are intruding. I am satisfying my own curiosity, is all."

"That is true." Uncle sounded cheerful. "But I am curious myself, and I do not wish to trudge the two miles back to the village. The house is here, David has told me it has a caretaker, we are his friends, and they at least might let us sit down for a few minutes."

Sophie could not argue with his logic. The spring day had turned warm and a rest would be welcome.

The door opened when Uncle rang the bell, revealing a tall footman who looked down his haughty nose at the dusty travelers.

"Good afternoon," Uncle said brightly. "I am Dr. Pierson, and this is my niece. We are great friends of Mr. Fleming." Uncle beamed at the footman who, to Sophie's surprise, softened.

"Ah, yes. Her Grace of Kilmorgan sent word. Please enter, sir. Madam."

Sophie prepared to follow her uncle inside when hoofbeats sounded behind them.

Up the side path, well out of the way of the more formal garden, galloped a horse and rider. The horse halted, and the rider, dressed in a sleek black suit complete with top hat, slid from the saddle, tossing reins to a groom who'd materialized to meet them.

The rider strode toward the house, head down, paying no attention to the visitors. He hopped over the railing onto the terrace without bothering with stairs, still not noticing his guests until he found them blocking the front door.

David stumbled to a halt, his gray-blue eyes widening, his chest lifting with a startled breath.

Sophie wanted to dissolve into mist and disappear. She'd been so very certain he wouldn't be here—Eleanor had assured her David rarely came home.

In the next heartbeat, David left behind shock and obvious dismay to become a congenial host. He removed his hat and rubbed the dust from his hair, giving them a warm smile.

"My dear friends, had I known, I'd have sent a coach to the station and extended a carpet when you arrived. I can't promise a buried Roman villa for you, Pierson, but I hope what little I have will delight."

David waved them into the house, out of the spring sunshine. His welcome included Sophie, but he didn't look at her.

The interior of the house was even grander than Sophie expected. The entrance hall rose two floors, its high ceiling painted with clouds and frolicking cherubs. Paintings hung on the paneled walls, many depicting the house and grounds, while others were portraits. Sophie at once found a painting of David along with that of an older man who, by the resemblance, must be his father. A woman with soft gray eyes peered from a painting next to his.

A few of the older pictures depicted men and women in Scottish dress, and on one wall hung a family tree, wonderfully curlicued and embellished, with small names written all over it.

Uncle Lucas, his valise taken by the footman, went at once to this. "Your ancestry?" he asked David.

David strolled to him, the world-weary man returning. "My pater was *very* proud of the fact that we are distantly related to the Dukes of Kilmorgan, ever since Angus Roland Mackenzie married Donnag Fleming, my great-great-something aunt. I have no real Mackenzie blood, only Mackenzie in-laws, as it were." He waved at paintings higher up the walls, difficult to see in the shadows. "The rest of the lot hanging here are the D'urbeys, who owned the property before the last scion lost his fortune at cards and died penniless. My father snapped up this property for a song after the Crown, who'd taken it back, didn't know what to do with it. He ever loved a bargain."

Sophie studied the names on the family tree, one branch leading from Malcolm Mackenzie, who fought in the '45, and his son Angus, down through the ages to Hart Mackenzie, the current Duke of Kilmorgan, Eleanor's husband. Names beneath Hart and his brothers had been written in—their wives and many children.

The other branch led from the brother of Donnag Fleming, unfolding down to David Fleming father, and David Fleming son.

"Fascinating," Uncle Lucas said in true interest. "Every name has a story behind it, I wager."

David looked pained. "They do, but nothing I am prepared to tell you now in the middle of the hallway after a long and dusty journey. If you are truly intrigued, I'll pair you up with Ian Mackenzie, who is an expert on the family history. He can relate the stories in great detail."

"That would be splendid." Uncle Lucas meant it, Sophie knew, and would likely hound David until he set the appointment.

"Now then, it is a poor host who keeps his guests in the draughty hall. Thomas will be scurrying about upstairs, harrying the rest of the staff to prepare rooms for you. You will of course stay, unless you plan to rush for the last train out?"

David sent them a look of mild inquiry, as though he didn't care one way or the other, but Sophie saw the uneasiness in his eyes.

"We will indeed stay, my dear fellow," Uncle Lucas said. "We had hoped for a billet here, though we were prepared to bed down in the village if need be. I believe Lady Eleanor telegraphed to your servants, so they will be more prepared than you fear."

"Eleanor?" David flashed a frown at Sophie. "I see."

He clearly did not, but before Sophie could stammer an explanation, Uncle continued in his exuberant way.

"I know you must think us rude, but I had a hankering to see your house and the gardens I've heard so much about. They are written up in newspapers, you know. Since you flit about so much, I thought we'd simply come on our own without bothering you."

Sophie stared as her uncle lied for her. He did it well, smiling gently, the vicar's collar on his throat giving his words credence.

"You had but to ask, my friend," David said. "I am glad you have come—it will keep supper from being a deadly dull and silent meal. When I'm home, I mostly eat with my valet, Fortescue, and read the newspaper, but I left the man in London. Thank heavens—he is forthright with his many opinions."

David spoke glibly, but Sophie sensed his tension. He did not want them there, had barely stopped himself from leaping back onto his horse and riding away when he found them on his doorstep.

"It was me," she blurted. Both men turned to her in astonishment, and Sophie's face scalded. "I wanted to see your house, Mr. Fleming. I was curious. Uncle traveled with me for propriety's sake."

David gazed at her for one endless moment, stillness shielding any emotion in his eyes, then his sardonic expression returned. "Ah, it is the *building* that holds the Pierson family interest, not the man who owns it. Well then, I'll leave you to have supper with my house, while I take something in my chambers. You'll never know I am here."

"Don't be ridiculous," Uncle Lucas said. "Of course we are delighted you are home. We didn't expect you, nor you us, but we are all good enough friends that none of it matters. Now, let us each refresh ourselves and meet again for supper—by then we will have all recovered our tempers."

David and Sophie stared at him. Uncle liked to be the most self-effacing gentleman possible, but when he decided to take charge, he could be a force of authority.

"Yes, Uncle," Sophie said meekly.

"Yes, Uncle," David echoed. He shot Sophie a glance, and winked.

———

PIERSON ALLOWED THEM ONLY CONGENIAL TOPICS AT supper that night, both to David's relief and frustration. The history of the house and its interesting inhabitants, the joy of the unusually warm weather, the design of the gardens—by none other than Capability Brown, of course—why the house had been built in the French style, and what sort of crops grew in David's fields.

Nothing about their impromptu visit, what David had been up to in London, Sophie's divorce, or David's triumph regarding her annulment.

Once conversation surrounding David's house had been exhausted, Pierson went on at length about the dig and his Roman villa. Dr. Gaspar had proved so competent that Pierson had been comfortable leaving the excavation in the man's hands for a few days. Though, he added with amusement, a villa of Roman Britain was a bit too modern for Gaspar's tastes.

Sophie also looked pleased with Dr. Gaspar's expertise, to David's irritation. He needed to speak with her.

"A stroll?" he suggested after the meal had finished. Light lingered in the sky even if a brisk breeze had sprung up.

Pierson brightened, then caught on that David meant a walk with Sophie alone. "A bit chilly for me," he said quickly. "I'd love a rummage through your library."

The efficient Thomas, in charge of the sparsely staffed house, led him off, Pierson chattering excitedly all the way. This left David to escort Sophie, once they'd fetched wraps, out to the terrace. David glanced at the lighted windows of the library, which showed Dr. Pierson avidly looking over books packed onto a tall shelf.

"I never knew he could dissemble so well," he remarked. "I suppose that's a good trait in a vicar."

"Yes, Uncle is full of surprises." Sophie's words were light but stiff.

David could think of nothing to reply so he led her unhurriedly down the steps to the main garden, where lingering twilight touched pale flowers.

"Beautiful in the summer," David said as they walked side-by-side, not touching. "Fountains play, birds sing, the trees are green. Absolute paradise. Or so I remember as a child."

"Do you not come here for summers now?" Sophie's face softened. "It is incredibly lovely. You are lucky."

"No, I'm usually flitting about Britain or the Continent, doing errands for Hart. All part of the game."

He heard weariness in his voice that he never meant to put there. Only a few years ago, he'd thrived on the game, chasing down men reluctant to help Hart with his schemes, campaigning for his own seat in Commons. What had changed?

"Well, one day you must come for the summer and enjoy it," Sophie said.

David halted. "Are you feeling quite well, Miss Tierney?"

Sophie turned from admiring the view. "Ever so robust. Why?"

"You aren't teasing me, twitting me, or telling me I'm an ungrateful wretch for throwing everything my father built to the wind."

Her faint smile made his heart turn over. "I don't need to. You've just done it yourself."

"And I'd say you are right."

Sophie stood very still, the night breeze stirring the curls on her forehead, peeping from under her fetching fur hat. "Is that why you rushed away to London? Something to do with your estate? And why you returned today?"

"Pardon?" David made himself cease watching the way Sophie's lips moved, which only enticed him to kiss them. "No, indeed. I went to London to see about your annulment."

All color left her cheeks. "You mean my divorce. Which I asked you to leave alone."

David faced her squarely. "I know you asked me, but of course I could not. And you will have an annulment. The solicitors have all the papers now and it only awaits the verdict of a judge."

CHAPTER 13

*S*ophie's breath left her, her lacings suddenly far too tight. She turned swiftly as she coughed, seeking air.

David was beside her in an instant. "My dearest Sophie, forgive this wretch for springing the news on you so callously. But it is the truth. We can rejoice."

Spots swam before Sophie's eyes, but she found her voice. "You are wrong. My husband will never let me go that easily."

"Oh, but he will. With the Scots Machine and Hart Mackenzie on your side, the proceedings will take mere weeks, not the months it does for lesser mortals."

"You don't know Laurie," Sophie said, shaking her head. "He does as he pleases, and he wants to humiliate me. I did not fill his nursery like the dutiful wife I was supposed to be. He is punishing me for that."

Somehow David's hand was on her arm, holding her up. "If I may say so, Lackwit underestimates me and Hart, not to mention Sinclair McBride. The marriage will be annulled, you may trust me on that. I'll spare you the sordid details—believe me, they are sordid—but Lackwit will keep his mouth shut to protect himself."

Sophie slid from his touch and began to walk, wandering down the darkening path toward the woods. She had no idea where she was going, but movement was better than standing still. At least she could breathe again.

David's warm body beside her cut the chill. Sophie knew she should make for the house, find Uncle and a fire, but her feet would not obey.

"I thought I'd make you happy," David was saying. "I might have known I had no power to do that."

Sophie slowed to a stop at the edge of the garden, where a line of trees divided the formal park and gardens from the fields beyond. Those fields were the real world, where farmers toiled and animals built burrows. Inside the garden was gentleness, sanctuary.

But not for David. When he'd sought peace, he'd traveled to Uncle's remote vicarage, in spite of the inconvenient trains, rather than come here. Why?

"I am grateful, in spite of what I seem," Sophie managed to say. "You are stirring powerful people to help me, for no gain to yourself. I don't know why you should help, except that you are a kind man, no matter how you protest to the contrary. But I'm so afraid, David. So afraid to hope."

David watched her in silence, his eyes a glimmer in the shadows. He went so still that Sophie touched his shoulder.

He started, then caught her hand. "I am afraid to hope too," he said softly. "Do you know? You've just addressed me as *David*."

Sophie began to shake. "I beg your pardon. I am agitated ..."

David put his finger to her lips. "I prefer it. Not Mr. Fleming. *David*. As though we are intimate." He came closer. "Sophie."

The darkness embraced them, and shadows hid them from the house. They were alone here, more than they had been on the hill by the abbey. Sophie's heart beat just as swiftly as it had then, his nearness sending her reason to the wind.

She rose on tiptoe and sought his mouth in a kiss.

She'd meant it to be a light touch, a reassurance that he was real, and with her. But as soon as their lips met, David's arms came hard around her and he dragged her close.

His heat enveloped her as his lips parted hers, his strength turning the kiss deep. As he swept his tongue into her mouth, hot need gripped her and would not let go.

She pulled him against her, wanting this kiss. She'd dreamed so often of being in this man's bed—imagined David's slow smile as he shed his clothes, firelight touching his strong body, his sure hands on her skin.

Her heart pounded, and she felt his hammering as hard. His hands were firm on her back, fingers splayed. The breeze turned cold, but David kept her warm.

Dizzily she broke the kiss but kept her hands on his shoulders. "I'm not ..." She shook her head, eyes stinging. "I'm not a free woman."

David gave her a feral smile. "If the marriage is proved invalid, that means you already are free. You never were married."

But then she'd be ruined, having shared a bed with a man who wasn't her husband. If she followed David's logic, however, being already ruined meant she had nothing to lose by becoming his lover.

She laughed shakily. "You are trying to make me as bad as yourself."

David touched her cheek. "No one, least of all your sweet self, could ever be as bad as I am."

"You wish to be irredeemable." Sophie gave him a tremulous smile. "Why?"

"I don't. But it's easier if I accept it. I am a bad, bad man and there is no help for me."

"You're wrong." Sophie laid her head on his shoulder, closing her eyes as he sheltered her in his arms. "You're a good man masquerading as a reprobate. Uncle would never be so fond of you otherwise."

"He's nostalgic for the youth I was when we first met." David's embrace tightened, and she felt his lips on her hair. "But to hear you believe in me makes me half-hope the devil within will flee. I will become a puddle of straight-laced virtue, if that will make you happy."

"I think that would be frightening."

His laughter vibrated her in a fine way. "I agree with you."

"Can virtue be a puddle anyway?"

"I have no idea. I've never been virtuous, so I couldn't say." David's voice dropped to a softness she hadn't heard in him before. "But I can promise you, I would never, ever hurt you. I'd never be such a fool."

Sophie wrapped the words around her. She wanted so much to be treasured by him, the way she'd once believed men treasured their wives. Her own parents were happy, and she'd naively thought all marriage like theirs. She'd believed magic would happen when she married Laurie, transforming him into the perfect husband.

She hardly believed now she'd been so innocent. A man like David Fleming would never have been let near her when she was a debutante, yet he was proving to have far more worth than the too-charming bachelor earl who'd been the correct man to marry.

"We should go inside." David's voice remained low but took on an edge. "Lest I do something even more devilish."

Sophie shivered agreeably. "Perhaps I wish you to be devilish."

David kissed the bridge of her nose. "Do not tempt me."

"I wish ..." She leaned into him, running her hand down his coat. The warm man beneath stirred, the rumble in his throat like a caress.

"I know what you wish. I wish it too." David cupped her cheek, turning her face up to his. "I want you, Sophie. Want you with an intensity that's killing me."

His next kiss told her he'd been containing himself until now. He dragged her up to him, his mouth searing as he opened hers. Sophie's head went back, David holding her upright as her knees weakened.

She felt his hand on her backside then her thigh, teasing her legs apart. He stepped between them, his hardness apparent through her skirts.

Here under the trees no one would see them. He could lift her, hold her against the bole of the large elm behind her, satisfy the ache that never let her rest.

"Please," she heard herself whisper.

David answered with another kiss, grip tightening. He wanted it as much as she did—his mouth, touch, and body told her this as loudly as if he'd shouted it.

The virtuous man he claimed he wanted to be would have pushed Sophie from him in shock, perhaps lecture her on propriety as he dragged her to the house. A bad man like David only kissed her harder, a groan in his throat.

"Dear God." David wrested his mouth from hers and stepped back, hands on her shoulders, fingers biting down. "Sophie, what the devil are we doing?"

"Being consumed with need?" Sophie tried to speak glibly, but she trembled so she could barely form words.

"Obviously. But if we do not walk sedately to the house, I will be carrying you back with our clothes in shreds, and your uncle will take a bullwhip to me. Never mind that he's a kind man—he has the wrath of God on his side."

Sophie shook her head, her hair tumbling. "He would never ..."

"Perhaps not literally, but he would cast me out. I want ..." David dragged in a breath. "I want everything to be right."

"The world isn't right," Sophie said sadly.

"I know. But I want to stand with you and face it. Not with us looking debauched and depraved."

Sophie let out a little sigh. "I am finding virtue not worth the trouble."

"I agree. But ..." David's eyes held sadness and resignation. "I refuse to save you only to ruin you. It cuts at me to wait, but I will."

It cut at Sophie as well. She was already ruined—did he not realize that? In the eyes of the world, it no longer mattered what Sophie did. Because of Laurie, she'd been painted as a whore, and that was the end of it.

David gently straightened her hat then put his arm around her and led her to the gardens, silence enveloping them.

Only the breeze spoke, the rushing sound in the branches like water, but it couldn't soothe Sophie's fire or troubled spirit.

———

For the first time in his life, David enjoyed a sojourn in his own house. He'd spent most of his adult life avoiding it, the memories too thick.

After his mother's death, his father, in grief and pain, had filled the house with mistresses and rakes. He'd hosted lavish entertainments that ran between puzzling to frightening to a small boy, from drunken routs to outright orgiastic gatherings.

David had found relief with school and friends, but he'd grown up surrounded by decadence and easily fell into that way of life himself.

Now, viewing his home through Sophie's eyes, he discovered the beauty in it. Though his father had been broken inside, he'd had unusually good taste in art and architecture.

Keeping himself away from Sophie was more difficult. David wanted to seize her and kiss her at every turn, slide her against the wall and drink his fill. He wanted to rid her of her clothes, slowly, a button at a time, and touch the body the falling fabric revealed.

Never in his life had he been so close to a woman he'd wanted, and yet neither of them removed a stitch. Madness.

The presence of Dr. Pierson helped. Pierson knew full well how David felt about Sophie, and yet he chatted cheerfully about inane things like what sort of farming David did here and the history of the village church.

David took Sophie and Dr. Pierson over the house, from the attics to the gallery of famous paintings, to the ballroom and parlors made to host kings.

"It's like you," Sophie said on the last day of their visit. She and David lingered on the terrace, in full view of Dr. Pierson in the library—that is, they would be if Pierson bothered to look up from his books and maps. "The house, I mean."

"In what way?" David glanced at the walls behind him, the mansard roof high above. "Pray tell. I do like a good metaphor."

Sophie gave him the smile he'd grown to love. She'd softened since her first night here, when she'd been brittle, fearing to believe the troubles in her life could ever be over.

But they would be. David would see to it.

"Outwardly hedonistic," Sophie said. "Bathing the senses in

sumptuous luxury, promising delights. But solid beneath, comforting. Steady. Peaceful."

"Steady and comforting." David huffed a laugh. "What every gentleman wants as his epitaph."

She gave him a look. "I know you are not offended, so do not pretend to be so."

"Nothing you do offends me, Sophie, love."

Their hands rested near each other's on the railing, hers slender in dark brown gloves, his hard in black leather. Their arms were nearly touching but not quite.

This waiting was horrible. And there was nothing to say that when Sophie found herself free she'd turn to David.

All he could do was see what would come. When foolish and young, he'd thrown himself at a woman, and he'd fallen on his face.

He refused to do that again.

Sophie said nothing more, but what he saw in her eyes told him the waiting was difficult for her too. He moved an inch closer, still not touching her, but sharing her warmth. They stood so, in silence, drinking in the night and each other, before Pierson emerged to rattle on about ancient methods used in these parts to till the earth.

The next morning, the Fleming coach pulled to the front steps to take Sophie and Dr. Pierson to the village station. David handed Sophie in.

"I thought you were coming with us," Pierson said in bewilderment as David stepped back once the vicar had settled himself. Sophie remained quiet—she, being more observant, had probably noted the footman loaded only the valise she and her uncle had brought with them. No bags for David.

"Things to do," David said. "Worry not, dear sir, I will turn up soon in Shropshire, clad in ragged tweed, ready to break my back for you once more. I have business to take care of. Trial to face and so forth."

Sophie sent him a worried look. "Mr. Griffin is still pursuing the suit?"

David had deliberately not spoken of his impending trial or Sophie's marriage since their first night. It had been pleasant to talk about houses and gardening, archaeology and local history. Who'd have known such topics could be so entertaining?

"He is, confound him." David kept his voice light. "Do not worry, my friends. Basher McBride will shred the prosecution and have Griffin on his knees abjectly begging my pardon."

Pierson nodded, believing him. Sophie looked more trepidatious, but David shut the coach's door, deliberately not touching the hand she lay on the windowsill.

Sinclair's last message had indicated that Griffin was out for blood. David had angered so many people in his life that he might well have to face the music now—Griffin had many supporters. David had confidence that Sinclair would win the day, but they might have to concede much to Griffin before the man backed off.

But facing a trial that might end in David breaking rocks at Dartmoor did not gouge him as much as saying good-bye to Sophie that day. He folded his arms over his chest to contain his emptiness, watching dust rise as his coach carried her down the drive and perhaps out of his life.

SOPHIE WENT THROUGH THE NEXT WEEKS WITH DIFFICULTY. Dr. Gaspar had continued with the dig, unearthing a stash of pottery that excited him and Uncle greatly. No gold or treasure could have made Uncle Lucas happier than these everyday cooking pots.

David remained absent. Sophie made herself cease scanning the road hopefully or rushing to the door of the vicarage when any cart rumbled by.

Eleanor did not return either, though she sent the developed photographs to Uncle Lucas and promised to take more when the London Season let her escape.

Sophie tried to shut out the world and concentrate on helping her uncle, but it was difficult. She found herself, during the tedious process of brushing dirt from the mosaic or the potsherds, thinking of nothing but David, how safe she'd felt in his arms, how decadent under his kiss.

His voice, his deep laughter, the scent of smoky wool and brandy, the gleam in his eyes before he launched into one of his satirical speeches.

He'd burned his way into her heart, and Sophie knew he'd not leave it soon.

Within a week, Sophie decided to tell Dr. Gaspar about her circumstances. He deserved the truth, and she preferred to tell him her story before he learned it from the newspapers or whispers in the village.

She explained to him over breakfast, with Uncle Lucas's approval. Dr. Gaspar listened with confusion in his brown eyes, and then sympathy. She included the fact that David claimed the marriage would end in annulment instead of divorce, but both events were a scandal, though the annulment was the lesser of the two evils.

Dr. Gaspar said little, to Sophie's relief. That is, until later, when she bent over pieces of pottery in Uncle Lucas's shed, trying to decide if any matched. The faint odor of cow lingered in the old byre, but it was faint enough to be a comforting, not off-putting, scent.

Dr. Gaspar filled the doorway, cutting off what little light had filtered inside. "Miss Tierney." He cleared his throat, looking uncomfortable in the confined space. "I mean—I think—Lady Devonport?"

"Miss Tierney will do well," Sophie said, sliding from the stool to her feet. "I suppose I had better become used to it. Is Uncle asking for me?"

She made for the door, wondering what task Uncle Lucas wished her to perform now, but Dr. Gaspar remained awkwardly in her way.

"I am grateful to you for taking me into your confidence, Miss Tierney." He cleared his throat again, agony in his eyes.

Sophie shrugged as though none of it—her life, her reputation, her future—truly mattered. "Not at all. I knew you would hear the gossip before long."

"It must be difficult for you."

She gave him a wan smile. "A bit. But I hope it will be finished soon."

"When it is ..." Dr. Gaspar removed his hat, wiped his forehead, and set the hat back on his head. He glanced at the pottery pieces, coughed, rubbed his hands together, and took off his hat again. "When it is, Miss Tierney, I hope that you will do me the honor of becoming my wife."

CHAPTER 14

Sophie stilled in astonishment, uncertain she'd heard aright. But no, Dr. Gaspar had just asked her to marry him and now waited in anxious anticipation for her answer.

"I beg your ..." Sophie clutched the edge of the table. "Your *wife?*"

Gaspar nodded, seeming to gather courage from his blurted proposal.

"I know it is a surprise. But it distresses me to think of you ruined and pushed aside. You are a lovely woman, if you forgive my forwardness, and intelligent too—I haven't met many ladies who know the difference between Ancient Babylon and Hellenistic Greece." He gave a breathy laugh. "You would be handy when I return to the Near East—a man with a helpmeet who knows how to sort pottery would be ..." He waved at the scattered pieces of clay. "Heavenly, I think."

Sophie felt the world spin beneath her, the walls of the shed wavering. "I don't ... I ..."

"I know I have sprung this upon you." Dr. Gaspar's lips quivered behind his thick beard. "But please contemplate my offer.

You've declared you will be your uncle's assistant, but I would hate to see you wasted as a spinster. You would regain respectability as a married woman—and a mother."

He averted his gaze and blushed painfully as he spoke the last word.

Sophie opened her mouth to point out that he'd need to overcome his bashfulness if he wanted her to bear his children, but she shut it again.

She could say such things to David, and he'd laugh. Tease her, yes, but he wouldn't faint in mortification. Dr. Gaspar might.

"You are very kind." Sophie made her voice firm. "But I have not decided what I will do."

"Of course, of course. You must wait for the courts." Dr. Gaspar paused, still anxious. "When the legal issues are behind you, you will give me your answer?"

Sophie hated to hurt people's feelings. Any idea that someone smarted inside because of her made her unhappy, but she understood that if she did not tell Dr. Gaspar the truth, he might persist for the next forty years. The archaeology world was small, and their paths would often cross.

"Forgive me," she said, standing as straight as she could. "But my answer must be no. As I say, you are kind ..."

Dr. Gaspar's crestfallen look was difficult to bear. He removed his hat and turned it in his hands. "I see." He chewed his upper lip. "You can give me no hope?"

Sophie shook her head. "I am sorry, but no. I pray you can forgive me, and we can continue to be friends."

"Yes, yes." He put on his hat again, pulling it down to his ears. "Beg pardon for disturbing you."

Dr. Gaspar turned to leave. Sophie was about to let out a breath of relief when he turned back. "When you are unmarried once more—though the words sound strange—I will speak to you again. I daresay you will change your mind when you find your-self alone."

He tipped his hat, though he had to scrape it from his head to do it, and finally slunk out.

Sophie sank to her chair with a thump. She supposed Dr. Gaspar thought himself charitable, but he assumed that when Sophie found herself without a husband, she'd leap at his offer— any husband would be better than none. Blast the man.

She wished David were here so she could tell him about the bizarre encounter. He *would* laugh, she was certain of it. He'd also understand why she'd turned Gaspar down. Though a woman in her situation might be tempted to marry a man who'd whisk her away from the condemning gaze of society, David would realize why she'd said no.

Not that David, for all his kisses and declarations, had offered her marriage. He'd blatantly suggested he wanted an affair with her, wanted her in his bed, but he'd never said a word about matrimony.

The potsherds blurred before her as tears filled Sophie's eyes and spilled to her cheeks.

DR. GASPAR'S PROPOSAL, AND SOPHIE'S REFUSAL, MADE THE next day or so decidedly awkward. Dr. Gaspar never said a word, but his gazes from his rather sad brown eyes conveyed much. Uncle, who knew nothing of the matter, spoke robustly about the dig and never noticed Sophie's silence or Dr. Gaspar's nervousness.

A letter from the Duchess of Kilmorgan, which reached Sophie a few mornings later, came as a welcome relief.

I would be grateful if you would be my guest in London,

Eleanor wrote. *The Season is reaching its height, and I've been abandoned by my sisters-in-law. Isabella has a large social calendar of her own with the art crowd, Ainsley has retreated to Berkshire with her husband for the horse season, and Beth lives a quiet life with Ian. My nephew Daniel's wife often helps me, but Violet and Danny are tinkering like mad with a motorcar, determined to win the latest time trial, whatever those are.*

If you could see your way to aiding me in my desperation, I would be unceasingly obliged to you. I will also be able to finish my duties quicker so I can take more photographs for your uncle, and no, I am not above a little bribery to bring you to my side. Also it would do you no harm to be seen outside your marriage and under my protection. I speak bluntly because nothing will move forward if I am too delicate to point out your precarious position, which I am not.

Most of all, I would enjoy spending time in your company. I find you refreshing, and my home rather over-runneth with gentlemen. They are fine fellows to be sure, but a female voice in the clamor is always welcome.

Do say you'll come. I will send my maid, who brooks no nonsense, to escort you, so that you will be saved the horrors of traveling in a train car by yourself. I have also sent the fare for a first class ticket enclosed in this letter, since I am demanding your presence.

Yours in haste,
Eleanor Kilmorgan

SOPHIE'S RIDE TO LONDON IN THE CUSHIONED LUXURY OF the first-class carriage, Eleanor's prim maid to look after the luggage, proved to be soothing. The maid sat upright in the opposite seat, darning socks, for the entire journey. Eleanor's sons ran through them quickly, it seemed.

Sophie's own lady's maid had given notice the moment Laurie's solicitor had informed Sophie of the divorce proceedings, and after so many months she found it disconcerting but comforting to have someone procure all tickets, snap orders for the luggage to be carried, and see that Sophie was taken care of all the way to Eleanor's front door.

They approached London from the north, Regent's Park green with spring. The park at Grosvenor Square was also tinged green, studded with nannies and children enjoying a spate of fine weather.

The Grosvenor Square home of the Duke of Kilmorgan was far grander than any London house Sophie had ever visited, including her husband's. The Earl of Devonport's townhouse paled against the double mansion with tall windows whose black fan-lighted door opened to a vast hall.

The lady of the house appeared on the landing of a lavish staircase in pursuit of two boys with red hair, both of whom hurtled toward Sophie with blood-curdling yells.

"Do catch him!" Eleanor shouted as the smaller of the pair shot toward the open front door, evading the footmen and the lady's maid who lunged to stop him.

Sophie stretched out her arms and caught up the child before he could race out into the street. He was heavy and squirming, but her heart warmed as she held him close and looked him in the face. "Good evening, little man. Where are you rushing off to? I've only just arrived."

The boy ceased struggling and stared at Sophie. He had blue eyes like his mother, his hair dark red, his face freckled.

"I'm Malcolm," he announced in a voice that carried to the

lofty ceiling. "Are you mum's friend come to stay? Do you play draughts? Or poker? Cousin Danny taught me."

"I am a mean one for draughts," Sophie promised. The door had been closed behind her so she set the lad on his feet.

The slightly older boy waited politely in front of Sophie. "I am Alec Mackenzie," he said, holding out his hand. "How do you do?"

Malcolm snorted. "Prissy-prissy."

"There's nothing wrong with good manners, Mal," Eleanor said as she came off the stairs.

Sophie shook Alec's hand solemnly, then said to Malcolm, "And of course I know how to play poker. My uncle taught me."

"See?" Malcolm yelled at Alec. He took a swing at his brother then bolted toward the back of the house.

Alec's formality dropped in an instant and he raced after Malcolm with a scream of a Highland warrior ready for battle. Two footmen, who must be charged with keeping the boys alive, hurried after them.

"You see why I find photographing ancient tiles in dark holes so refreshing," Eleanor said to Sophie. "Alec is home from school for a short holiday, and there has been no silence in the house since." In spite of her words, the look she turned to the vanishing boys held so much love that Sophie's heart squeezed.

"They are lovely children."

"They are little hellions," Eleanor said. "Like their father and uncles. But yes, quite lovely." She patted Sophie's arm and smiled. "How wonderful that you've come. We will have a fine time, I know it."

ELEANOR KEPT SOPHIE IN SUCH A WHIRL OVER THE

following weeks that she scarcely distinguished one day from the next. They planned soirees, musicales, and garden parties—bringing the garden parties indoors if the weather did not cooperate.

When not hosting her own gatherings, Eleanor took Sophie with her to balls and suppers, the theatre, and the opera. During daylight hours they visited museums and libraries and met other ladies for tea.

Sophie was trepidatious about these outings at first, but Eleanor's friends—who must have been hand-picked to make Sophie comfortable—welcomed her into their circle. Among these were Eleanor's sisters-in-law, Isabella, Ainsley, and Beth, and Hart's niece Violet, none of whom seemed to be as busy as Eleanor's letter had suggested. Sophie especially liked Violet, an intelligent young woman, very much in love with her husband, with a knack for mechanical devices.

All these ladies had been touched by scandal or the dark side of life, Sophie learned—Beth had grown up in a workhouse; Isabella had eloped with Mac Mackenzie on the night of her come-out; Ainsley had been seduced at a very young age; and Violet had been a faux stage medium to make a living, though she claimed that her mother appeared to have a true gift for clairvoyance.

The McBride wives—sisters-in-law of Ainsley—who rounded out the group had similar stories, and Louisa, Isabella's sister, had fallen so low as to marry a policeman. This last was told to Sophie with merriment—Detective Superintendent Fellows was no mere policeman.

None of these ladies found the impending breakup of Sophie's marriage scandalous at all. They surrounded her on outings, befriending her in truth, and kept more unforgiving members of society away from her. With the Duchess of

Kilmorgan and the ladies Mackenzie at Sophie's side, no one dared to shun her.

Eleanor had said she'd protect Sophie, and protect her she did.

The one person Sophie never saw on these rounds was David.

"He's still in Hertfordshire," Eleanor told Sophie when Sophie finally summoned the courage to inquire about him. "He is not supposed to come to London, according to Fellows—not that it stops him. But he's being careful. I'm very glad to see it. David is finally taking his position as landed gentleman seriously. He has been a loyal friend to Hart all these years, but good heavens, David needs his own life."

Sophie remembered the cozy evenings she'd spent in David's home, the camaraderie from the vicarage almost renewed. Not quite—there had been a strain since the night he'd kissed her so passionately at the edge of the garden. Even so, Sophie thought longingly of those evenings around the fire, talking of anything and everything.

David accepted Sophie for who she was, a rare gift, she was coming to understand. She missed him.

Interestingly, ladies of the London ton had heard about Uncle Lucas's find of the Roman villa in Shropshire. Stories about it had been printed in several newspapers, including the *Illustrated London News*.

At a garden fete at a house in Mount Street one afternoon, Sophie heard both her uncle's name and David's in conversation. Pretending indifference, she wandered toward the ladies speaking about them, as though only admiring the hostess's lovely spring flowers.

"Griff is frightfully doleful," one woman in a dull lavender gown said. "He is unhappy about appearing in court, but that awful Mr. Fleming *did* try to kill him."

"I heard Mr. Fleming denies it with every breath," another lady said brightly.

"He would," the first woman said. "But my Griff says Mr. Fleming *shot* at him and then punched him in the face when the shot missed. Horrible. Mr. Fleming was arrested but then allowed to retreat to the country."

Sophie surmised that the first woman was *Mrs.* Griffin, and Griff, the man who'd accused David of attempted murder.

"I heard Mr. Fleming helped Dr. Pierson reveal the Roman villa in Shropshire," another lady said. "It was in the newspapers."

"So unfair," Mrs. Griffin said. "The *Illustrated London News*, no less. They barely sniffed when Griff found that Saxon gold in Suffolk. He offered to fund a full excavation, but no one would take it. Griff sits in his chamber, running his hands through the coins he turned up, quite morose. This trial will upset him too much. Mr. Fleming should admit guilt and go quietly to prison."

Sophie thought David should do nothing of the sort, but the exchange gave her an idea.

She continued across the garden as though seeking the shade of the house, but once inside, she excused herself to the hostess, returned to Eleanor's home, and asked the duke's butler to dispatch several urgent telegraph messages for her.

"TELEGRAM FOR YOU, SIR."

Fortescue, tall with his graying hair brushed to cover the thin spot on top of his head, bent down with a salver in his hand, an envelope squarely in its center. He enjoyed playing the perfect servant, complete with white gloves and upper-crust accent.

David lounged deep in a chair with his nose in a book about farming a vegetable called a swede. It was unbelievably technical. He'd always thought one dug a hole, dropped in a seed, and walked away, to pluck up the fully grown vegetable in the fall. But things such as the soil's content and consistency, average rainfall in the county, and field drainage apparently were all very important if a man wanted a fine crop of rutabagas.

At Fortescue's words, David happily shoved the book onto a table without bothering to mark his place.

"Miss Tierney has sent for me, declaring her undying love," he said in hope.

Fortescue looked down his nose. "I believe the message came from London, sir. From your solicitor."

"My solicitor?" David's light mood evaporated. "Not McBride, my barrister?"

"No, sir. I imagine Mr. Basher McBride is too busy to send his own telegrams."

"Cheek. But you are no doubt right. Then it is either to do with my trial or some other tediousness." David eyed the envelope on the tray with distaste. "Read it to me, Forty. My eyes are glazed by my intense study of soil composition."

Without a word, Fortescue set down the salver, slit the envelope with a silver knife he kept about his person, slid out the missive, unfolded it, and cleared his throat.

"I am pleased to report that Mr. Griffin has withdrawn all charges of assault and attempted murder," Fortescue read in a monotone. "The Crown has dropped the prosecution, citing lack of evidence."

hat?" David came to his feet, his mouth hanging open.

"All restrictions on your movements have been lifted," Fortescue finished. "Congratulations, sir." He didn't change expression, but David had known the man long enough to see the relief in his eyes.

David snatched the paper from Forty's hand. He read the message through—the words indeed said he no longer had to worry about Griffin and his accusations.

"How?" He demanded of the page, then he raised his head. "No—I don't care how. This changes everything. Pack my bags, Fortescue. We are racing to London tonight."

"London?" Fortescue's brows climbed the faintest bit, his version of excitement. "I've only just come from there."

"Well, we are going back. The swedes will have to wait."

"It is too early to plant them in any case," Fortescue said.

"Is it?"

Fortescue neatly folded the telegram David had dropped on the book and slid it back into the envelope. "Yes, sir. They prefer soil that is above forty degrees Fahrenheit, and my almanac says we will have several more frosts before the weather warms."

David dragged his thoughts back from Sophie's beautiful smile and focused on Fortescue's bland countenance. "How the devil do you know that?"

"I have had a lifetime to read as many books as possible, sir. When I understood that your interest had shifted, at long last, to what is growing in your own fields, I refreshed my knowledge of crops that thrive in this part of England. In case you had questions about them."

David laughed. "Forty, you are the most impertinent, presumptuous manservant I've ever had the misfortune to be saddled with."

"So you have said many times, sir. But as I am the *only* manservant you have ever been saddled with, the comparison can hardly exist."

"It is my way of saying I love you, Fortescue. Now, let us have those damned bags packed. I have a lady to woo. She'll turn me down flat, I'm certain, and soon I'll be back, trying to soothe my broken heart with research on fertilizer and crop rotation."

"She might say yes, you know," Fortescue said as David charged from the library to the stairs. "Then you can read to her all about tilling the fields. She will never regret her choice."

"Ha. She already thinks me the greatest fool in Christendom. Besides, she's still married at present, not to mention far more interested in Roman ruins than a ruined Englishman."

"Very poetic, sir."

"I thought so." David caught his breath at the top of the stairs. "A few small bags are all I need. Come and watch a lady trample me into the dust." He beamed at his long-suffering valet. "I cannot wait to see her."

SOPHIE STOOD ON A STOOL IN HER BEDCHAMBER WHILE Eleanor's dressmaker pinned a skirt in place, making tiny marks on it with chalk.

Eleanor had insisted Sophie have new dresses made, nothing drab or nondescript, she said severely—Sophie had nothing to be ashamed of. Thus, within a short time, Sophie found herself attired in deep blue silk evening gowns, bottle-green walking dresses, and dusky pink tea gowns.

Why Eleanor thought Sophie needed yet another ballgown, she wasn't certain, but Eleanor had rattled off a long explanation that Isabella had insisted it be done for the grand ball at the Grosvenor Square house and Sophie could not be seen in something she'd worn before. The Queen and the south of France had come into the speech somehow, and before Sophie could do more than blink, the dressmaker had arrived. Now Sophie stood in her underthings while swaths of silk enfolded her body.

Eleanor swept in, her blue eyes alight, her smile wide. "Mr. McBride is here. Dear Sinclair. He is so happy now that he has Bertie and more little ones. His eyes are softer, though not, I gather, when he is in court with a criminal squirming on the dock before him. He wants to see you—it must be to do with your marital state. I told him you'd be down at once."

The dressmaker, no doubt used to Eleanor's abrupt ways, began to calmly unpin the skirt. Eleanor assisted, apologizing profusely to the dressmaker and promising that Sophie would be back to continue the fitting forthwith.

Sophie restored her everyday skirt and shirtwaist, but her fingers shook so that Eleanor and the dressmaker had to help with her buttons. Eleanor hooked her arm through Sophie's and led her out, patting her hand as they descended the stairs. Sophie had thought to explain she could face Mr. McBride alone, but then decided against it. A friend at her side was just what she needed.

She was glad she hadn't insisted Eleanor leave her when they entered the front parlor. Mr. McBride, a handsome blond Scotsman, came to his feet at their entrance, but he wasn't alone. Next to him, already standing, was David.

Sophie's breath left her. David's gaze was all for her, his blue-gray eyes filled with his biting wit and a strange apprehension.

Eleanor stopped, as surprised as Sophie. "David, what are you doing here? The majordomo didn't announce you. Did you slide in under the moldings?"

David gave her a bow. "I bade your good man not to say a word. I was afraid neither of you would darken the door if you knew I lurked. I had rushed to London to visit McBride about my own situation, and he declared himself on his way to visit you. Naturally, I invited myself along. He has news."

Sinclair shot him a look. "They likely discerned that from my presence alone."

"Tell her." David folded his arms and stepped back, rocking restlessly on his feet.

Sinclair opened a case that lay on the table next to him and withdrew a long document, folded lengthwise. "I am pleased to inform you that Lord Devonport has been granted an annulment to his marriage to Miss Sophie Tierney. The marriage is declared invalid and nonexistent, and both parties are at liberty to marry another if they so choose."

Sophie's jaw loosened, and the next thing she knew, she was in a chair, Eleanor and David on either side of her. David shoved a glass under her nose, and Sophie inhaled the sharp bite of whisky.

"Drink it," David advised. "Trust me. Down it in one go."

David had to steady the glass for her, but Sophie obeyed.

Whisky filled her mouth, and she forced herself to swallow. Liquid burned fire down her throat but it settled her roiling stomach and let her draw a breath, her vision clearing.

Sinclair gazed upon her in sympathy. "Forgive me for springing it on you so abruptly, Miss Tierney. Barristers can be sharp, so my wife likes to tell me." His expression softened a long way when he said *my wife.*

"Not at all." Sophie tried to speak briskly, but her voice was breathy and wrong. "I needed to know. But ... are you certain? Laurie—or rather, his solicitors—told me he could not annul the marriage, and that divorce was the only way he could be rid of me."

David's hand tightened on hers before she realized he'd been holding it. Warm, anchoring David.

"I'd never have brought this to you if I weren't certain." Sinclair held up the papers and then laid them carefully on a table. "The marriage has been annulled on the grounds of physical incapacity."

Sophie blinked. "Physical ..." Bile touched her throat, and she longed for another gulp of the whisky. "You mean my inability to carry a child."

"By no means—"

David cut off Sinclair's gentle answer. "Not on your part, love. On Lackwit Laurie's. The evidence finds your husband incapable of siring an heir, a spare, a daughter, or anything else. Of completing the act at all. His soldier is always at ease, and by about ... oh, now ... several unscrupulous journalists will be announcing this fact to the world, using very circumspect wording and no names so they can't be charged with libel."

Sophie's mouth hung open again. She shut it with a snap. "You did this," she said rapidly to David. "*You* did all this."

"I did." David raised her hand to his lips, then he released her. "I am a monster. You may hate me for the rest of your life for making a complete fool of your husband and a mockery of your marriage. But I would do it again." His voice turned hard. "What matters is that you are free of him—free to choose your life, without a shadow of disgrace."

"Annulment is still a scandal," Sophie said, voice weak.

"Usually, yes," Eleanor's brisk tones broke in. "But with your husband declared impotent, it means that, in the eyes of the world, you are untouched, unsullied. Perhaps unwise in your choice to marry him in the first place, but everyone knows about Lackwit Laurie. He's a charmer with nothing behind the charm. You will be quite forgiven, and also unstained."

"But he isn't ..." Sophie swallowed and turned a dazed face to Sinclair. "Laurie isn't ..."

Sinclair held up his hand. "Say nothing. Never, ever say anything about it again, Miss Tierney, especially not to a man of law. Accept the verdict and carry on."

"Best way," Eleanor agreed.

Sophie swung to her, suspicions sharpening. "*You* knew, didn't you? You knew what David was up to."

"Well, of course." Eleanor looked serene. "He asked for my help. I thought it a delicious scheme and naturally agreed. I will not explain all the underhandedness, but you did not deserve to be married to that awful man, and as David says, I would do it again. Though *I* am not as contrite as he appears to be at the moment. Ladies can be much more ruthless than gentlemen, I always say."

They had all known. Sophie's gaze went from one to the other—Sinclair with compassion but warning caution, Eleanor gleeful, David grim. David had known the entire situation would disconcert her, but he had no regret over his part.

Somehow Mr. Fleming had convinced a barrister, a slew of

solicitors, and a judge of the courts that the Earl of Devonport was incapable of performing in bed. How David had proved such a thing, Sophie could not fathom, nor was she certain she wanted to.

He was duplicitous and determined—that much she understood. Somehow David had threatened Laurie enough that Laurie had agreed to the annulment and set Sophie free.

Sophie rose, her limbs stiff. David caught her arm, ready to assist, but she slid away from him, finding strength once more.

"I thank you, sir," she said, surprised her voice was steady. "You have done me a great service."

David's eyes flickered with pain. "It was my most profound pleasure." His throat moved in a swallow. "You deserve to be happy, Sophie. To have that chance."

Sophie made herself nod. "But just now I need ... I must ..."

She had no more words. Her dry eyes burned as she turned abruptly from David, waved off Eleanor's solicitous movement, and fled the room.

***

"I HAD THE FEELING SHE WOULDN'T FLING HERSELF INTO MY arms and cover me with kisses," David said despondently.

"Give her a moment." Eleanor accepted the whisky Sinclair handed her before he dispensed one to David. "This is a shock for her, however welcome."

David sank into a chair, unaccountably weary, and downed his whisky, as he'd advised Sophie to, in one dose.

Sinclair gave him a stern look. "If she discovers that courtesans were happy to do you a favor, Fleming, it might not appease her."

"I'll keep mum," Eleanor said. "Promise."

"No." David sighed from the depths of his boots. "I will tell her all. Eventually. She deserves to know every horrible lie and my hand in them."

"I see." Sinclair resumed his seat. "You wish to make certain she hates you thoroughly."

"So you can wallow in your broken heart and drive your friends distracted," Eleanor put in. "You do not always have to be a martyr, David. From the number of times Sophie has asked me about you since her arrival—then pretends to forget asking and inquires again—I would say the lady is smitten."

"My optimistic El." David heaved himself from the chair to refill his glass. He lifted it to drink, thought about the rivers of whisky that had run through his body in his life, and clicked the glass to the sideboard. "I might have saved her from dire scandal but I did it by no honorable means, and she knows it. Can she be comfortable with such a man as me? I will depart, and she will become the toast of London and marry some lucky gentleman within the year. She will have many children and grow old and happy."

Which she deserved. So why did David feel hollow inside?

"No, you don't." Eleanor was on her feet, facing him. "You will not run away, my friend. I helped you not only for *her* sake, but for yours. The devil I will let you retreat to the country like a wounded bear, becoming a hermit for unrequited love. Absolute nonsense. There is no reason for either of you to pine away alone. You will remain in London, and you will attend my supper ball, if I have to have Fortescue tie you up and drag you to it. He would, if I asked him."

"I know," David said gloomily.

"It might help you to know exactly *why* you are no longer facing charges from Mr. Griffin," Eleanor said, her eyes flashing.

She had no idea how frightening she was when she did that. Explained why Hart was a quiet man these days.

"Would it?" David asked. "I can't imagine what it has to do with Sophie's life."

"Please explain, Sinclair, there's a good fellow." Eleanor turned in a swirl of skirts and plopped into a chair to enjoy the waters she'd just stirred. Eleanor was a master at that.

Sinclair steepled his fingers. "I was prepared to explain when you arrived today, but understandably you were more interested in my visit to Miss Tierney, and prevented me. I will tell you that Mr. Oliver Griffin is now the principal funder and director of Miss Tierney's uncle's excavations of his Roman villa in Shropshire."

David stared at him. "What the devil? Why on earth is Griffin—?"

"Dr. Pierson will need money, a mountain of it, if he's to do this thoroughly," Sinclair interrupted. "I imagine Pierson hoped his old university would sponsor him, but a small villa of the Roman British period, even with an intact mosaic floor, has not drawn much attention. Mr. Griffin, as director of the excavations, will oversee the project, find donors, and possibly interest a museum or his Oxford college. *His* uncle, a vastly wealthy man, has already promised some funding. Mr. Griffin will no doubt take all credit for this project, though I did tell him that Dr. Pierson must be named as its primary discoverer. Mr. Griffin complied, and agreed to drop all charges against you for this carrot I extended him."

David groped at the back of a chair and moved himself to sit in it before his legs gave way.

"*You* offered it. How the devil did you know he'd want Pierson's dig? *Why* would he?"

"Miss Tierney told me." Sinclair spoke calmly but his gray

eyes betrayed vast amusement. Confounding David apparently entertained him.

"Miss Tierney—Sophie—told you ..."

"Do not speak as though she hasn't a brain in her head," Eleanor broke in. "She gathered the intelligence that Griffin is terribly interested in archaeology and greatly disappointed when no one wanted the Saxon antiquities he found in a burial mound in Suffolk. I suspect he is more interested in being lauded and celebrated than doing the actual work, but no matter. Sophie made inquiries, discovered that Griffin has found other burials and been rebuffed as a dilettante several times. She asked Dr. Pierson if he'd consider letting Griffin step into his dig—if he brought piles of cash with him, of course—and Dr. Pierson was delighted. Sophie then asked Sinclair to contact Griffin and offer this exchange."

Sinclair nodded, infuriatingly calm. "Mr. Griffin proved to be more interested in heading a dig than prosecuting a man for pummeling him."

David's lips were numb. "You knew this," he said to Eleanor. "I was festering in the country reading up on *root vegetables,* and you could not tell me my sentence would be lifted?"

Eleanor did not look the least bit contrite. "Sinclair and I decided it would be best if you knew nothing until he could present it to you as a fait accompli. If Griffin refused us at the last, you'd have been devastated and perhaps taken a foolish step —left the country or shot Griffin in truth, or some such."

"You know I'm not a violent man," David said, affronted. "Unless I'm powerfully drunk, which I haven't been in a long time. Not since—"

Not since he'd raised his head at Pierson's breakfast table and seen Sophie's extraordinary green eyes studying him in curiosity.

"Sophie." The very name soothed his senses. She'd found a

way to ease his troubles even when she'd been uncertain hers would ever vanish.

David sprang up, his energy returning. "I must go to her."

He rushed for the door, but found Eleanor in front of him.

"Not yet." Eleanor put a firm hand on his arm. "Give her time to let her changed situation sink in. She cannot go from being a married woman, however unhappily, to a single one in a heartbeat without some disturbance. She needs to find her equilibrium. Let her alone until my supper ball, which is three nights from now. I expect you to turn up, as I said, dressed in your finest."

David gazed down at the woman who'd once broken his heart. Broke it, stomped on it, and then offered her hand and asked to be friends. A formidable woman, and a good one. Hart Mackenzie was a lucky man, but Eleanor belonged with him. She never had with David. Good thing she'd been so sensible all those years ago.

"God bless you, El." The last dregs of David's lethargy burned away. He took Eleanor's hands and kissed her cheek. "You are too damned good to me. I will do as you command." He grinned. "You are also terrifying. Small wonder Hart looks pale." He kissed her cheek a second time and darted around her, avoiding her half-hearted swing. "Adieu, my friends." He turned at the door and made a flourishing bow to her and Sinclair, the tall, quiet barrister who'd stood by him through it all. "And thank you. I am a most favored man."

With that, he left them, his head full of plans, his heart light.

CHAPTER 16

Sophie had never worn such a gown before. Made of rippling pink and green silk, it swept from a tight bodice to a flowing skirt, gathered in back with a knot of cloth roses. The bodice was cut a bit lower than she was used to, and very snug in the waist, its sleeves whispers of gauzy silk. Her washed and brushed hair was piled on her head in wonderful curls, a few of which cascaded to her shoulders. A simple necklet of pearls completed the costume. Isabella, to whom the Mackenzie ladies turned for all things fashion, had said the necklet was enough.

Sophie agreed. Already news of her annulment had spread through Town, and people stared as she moved about the ballroom. Always best to look elegant when one was the subject of all attention.

Too many tonight asked her, "What will you do now?"

Sophie had no idea. Simply breathing was enough.

She privately concluded she'd return to her uncle's in Shropshire, not to hide, but to do something a bit more interesting than the same round of gatherings with the same people night after night.

As for the man responsible for her annulment...

She had not seen him. David had remained absent since the day Sinclair brought her the papers, and Eleanor had stated bluntly that she'd told him to leave Sophie be.

Wise, Sophie thought as she drifted through the crowd, a gracious smile on her stiff lips. The stares and sometimes blatant pointing unnerved her, but she kept her head high.

She suspected she would have made a grand fool of herself if David had returned to the house in the intervening days. She'd have flung her arms around him and covered him with kisses then backed away and shouted at him. And then rushed at him for more kissing.

She wanted more than that—if David had turned up, she might have torn his clothes from his body. She wanted to touch him, to kiss his skin...

Better to shout at him. He'd saved her and made her an object of fascination, pity, and amusement at the same time. She'd heard the whispers of *Limp-Prick Laurie* during her outings with Eleanor in the last few days, seen the sympathetic glances from the same whisperers. Laurie, it was rumored, had taken a sudden journey to the Continent. The widow he'd wished to marry rather abruptly turned her attentions to another.

The ballroom Sophie moved through—quickly enough that none could engage her in conversation—was full. Eleanor had invited most of the polite world tonight, presenting Sophie to them as Miss Tierney.

The Mackenzie brothers, tall Scotsmen in formal kilts, mingled with the guests. Hart busied himself being the important man he was—*making everyone dance to his tunes*, Eleanor had murmured to her while gazing at him in open affection.

Cameron, the tallest of them, spoke animatedly about horses to a fascinated group. Ainsley stood near him, adding to the conversation, her love for her husband obvious.

Mac Mackenzie laughed loudly with his cronies, his charm in evidence. He drank lemonade, as did Isabella at his side. They were a vibrant and lovely pair, warming all around them.

Daniel Mackenzie, young and exuberant, led his wife about with apparent pride. Violet was a beautiful woman, with whom Sophie had already become friends. Their baby daughter, Fleur, was tiny and sweet.

Sophie had only briefly met Ian Mackenzie, the brother those outside the family regarded as mad. Ian didn't look mad to Sophie as he walked through the crowd with Beth at his side, both of them calm and quiet. True, Ian did not engage in lively conversation like his brothers, but he did speak to people, usually after listening to them a time before breaking in with an apt observation.

Three of the McBride brothers had come as well—the fourth, Stephen, was with his regiment and his wife in Africa. Patrick and Rona, the patriarch and matriarch of the family, older than the others, were having a fine time. They'd raised the younger McBrides, Ainsley had told her. Sinclair had brought his wife, a merry-faced lady called Bertie. Sophie knew she'd started life in an East End gutter, but she was as stylish and gracious as any lady here, even if she winked at Sophie behind their backs.

Elliot McBride was quieter, but devastatingly handsome. More than one woman looked his way, but his wife, Juliana, at his side, was the only lady that held his gaze.

Sophie tried to calm her agitation by watching the Mackenzies and their friends, keeping herself to herself as much as she could without snubbing Eleanor's guests.

Until, that is, a knot of people at the end of the room parted, and she saw David standing near a long window that led to the garden.

The window was closed against the night's chill, its panes reflecting the chandeliers and the broad-shouldered man in black frock coat and Scottish kilt. He looked straight at Sophie.

Sophie's heart pounded as she drank in his hard body, the way the kilt hugged his hips. She'd never seen David in Scottish dress before, and she decided it much suited him.

A couple making their way to the dance floor nearly ran into her, and Sophie skittered aside with an apology. She realized she could no longer be a stone, and forced her satin-slippered feet toward the window. The distance was only a dozen yards in truth, but it felt like miles.

David watched her come, making no attempt to go to her. She had no idea how he would receive her—was he angry at her for not sending word to him? Or indifferent about their time apart?

"Good evening," she managed when she halted an arm's length from him. So she might say to any acquaintance.

"Good evening." David ran his blue-gray gaze up and down her, making her blood burn. "Lovely gown."

"Isabella chose it. You look ..." Sophie faltered, biting off her true words. *Delectable, beguiling, desirable.*

David spread his arms, a hint of his wicked smile returning. "Hart insists on a show of force from his Scottish cousins. Great-great aunt Donnag might have married a Duke of Kilmorgan, but her brother, my direct ancestor, married an Englishwoman. Hart barely forgives me for that, but if I bring out the kilt once in a while, he lets me be."

Sophie hid a nervous smile. "He is fond of you."

David glanced at the large Mackenzie who was holding his audience in thrall. "Perhaps. I've been loyal to him, if nothing else."

"They are all very fond of you." Sophie's speech was stilted, her words polite, as though she spoke to a man she barely knew. "I've been living in this house for a while now, and your name comes up often."

David's eyes flickered. "That is alarming."

"Not at all. The ladies speak of you highly. The gentlemen too."

"Even more alarming. I wonder what they want me to do for them?"

Sophie's amusement bubbled up, dissolving some of the tension inside her. "Must you always mock yourself?"

"Mocking myself makes others' mockery easier to bear."

She softened. "You are a fine man, David Fleming."

His restlessness quieted as he studied her face. The room behind Sophie seemed to fade, the music and chatter muted.

"My life will be worth living if you truly believe that," he said. "Damnation, Sophie, I wanted to come to you, to see you, to make certain you were well ..."

"Eleanor told me she kept you away." Sophie slid closer to him, unable to stop herself. "I wanted to see you too. To thank you ..."

"No." David held up his hands, his voice taking on a savage note. "I do not want your thanks or gratitude. It's not what I want from you." He closed his eyes briefly then gave himself a shake. "I am supposed to be thanking *you* for deflecting Griffin. How the devil you managed it, I don't know, but I liked learning that you are as devious as I am."

Sophie shrugged, the gauze of her sleeves rubbing her shoulders. "I overheard an interesting bit of conversation that made me ask questions, is all. I was glad to find the one thing Mr. Griffin wanted more in life than taking vengeance on you."

"Exactly." David's snake-like grin returned. "How do you

suppose I work the magic I do? If I could take you under my wing and teach you—ah, what havoc we could wreak!"

Sophie couldn't stop her laugh. "We'd be feared the length and breadth of England."

"Scotland too. It would be delightful." David's amusement faded. "Except it's hell to pretend you only a friend when you are standing so close to me, in that dress."

"Where should I stand? And in what frock?" She left off teasing. "I am proud to call you friend, David."

"You were not when you first saw me, a wreck of a man. I thank you for dragging me from that, if nothing else."

Her hands were in his before she realized she'd reached for them.

"I was as much of a wreck," she said. "Hiding from the world."

"Hiding with you was the best time of my life," David said fervently. "Far, far better than being in the world without you."

Sophie squeezed his hands. "I agree."

Music swelled behind them, reminding Sophie that they stood in Eleanor's ballroom, and that she was there to be reintroduced to society. She half-turned, ready to suggest they join the throng, when David pulled her back.

"Come with me," he said in a low voice.

Sophie felt no qualm about abandoning the ball to follow David. He led her around a screen that concealed a door to a narrow corridor—a passage for servants. David took her through this then up two flights of deserted backstairs before he opened another door into an upper hall.

Sophie's bedchamber lay nearby, but David towed her to a part of the house she hadn't visited and to a well-furnished bedchamber. The bedroom did not have the sumptuousness of the chamber Sophie occupied, but it was cozy, with a four-poster bed and well-cushioned chairs, a deep rug, and a crackling fire.

"Whose room is this?" Sophie asked in surprise. "And should we be invading it?"

"It is mine, dear lady. Set aside for me long ago, when Hart and I spent many nights in this house planning to take over the world." David gazed about in nostalgia. "Fortunately for the world, we did not succeed."

"They keep the fire lit for you?" Sophie wandered toward it, nervous. "Very considerate, since you are not staying here."

"I tipped the wink to the majordomo that I might spend the night. He is used to me getting roaring drunk at Hart's gatherings and having to be carried to bed."

Sophie made a show of looking him up and down. "You seem relatively sober."

"I am. Stone-cold. I certainly didn't want to come to you fluid with whisky. I've already done that, and seen you despise me."

Sophie flushed. "I was very rude." She remembered David looking up at her at her uncle's table with his changeable eyes, and her heart constricting. She'd blurted out her tart observations to hide her confusion.

"You were astute," David said. "I was a drunken sot. Could have saved myself much trouble that night if I hadn't been. But then, I might not have met you."

He joined her as she drew near the fire, taking her hands and pulling her close, his warmth competing with that of the flames.

David's smiles were gone, the lines on his face deepening as he gazed down at her. Firelight touched his dark hair and softened his hard-edged eyes.

Sophie rose on tiptoes to kiss the side of his mouth.

David made a raw noise in his throat. He released her hands to cup her face, drawing her up to him for a fierce kiss. His mouth moved on hers, hot, needing, and Sophie kissed him back with as much hunger.

David pulled away, eyes haunted. "Staying away from you has been hell, but I can't make myself keep from you any longer. If you want to run from me ..." He stepped back, the movement rigid. "I won't impede you. The door is unlocked, the way open. Go, and save your virtue from the likes of David Fleming."

Sophie studied him for a long time. David breathed hard, chest rising sharply, a pain in his eyes she felt in her own heart.

She moved from him and crossed the room. She heard David's sigh of resignation, almost a groan, before she quietly turned the key in the lock.

"Sophie." He gazed at her in such anguish it stabbed at her, but the hope behind his pain was even more anguished.

Sophie went to him. She closed her hands around the lapels of his coat, pulled him down to her, and kissed him hard on the mouth.

CHAPTER 17

$\mathcal{D}$avid's world changed. Sophie Tierney was in his arms, the scent of her light perfume filling him. Her gown bared her arms and back, her skin smooth under his callused hands.

Her mouth was a place of heat, like light brushing into him and freeing his dark heart. He pulled her closer, his body hard with wanting, drinking in the delight of her.

Her expression as she'd turned from the door had shattered him. She'd locked them in, coming to him willingly, to give him the gift of herself.

Thank all that was holy David had persuaded the major-domo have a fire laid. It warmed them now as they sought each other, the flickering light turning Sophie's dark hair to glistening silk.

David skimmed his hands down her back, finding the hooks that kept her bodice in place. He eased them apart as he continued the kiss, expecting at any moment she'd pull away from him and flee. Well, he'd left the way to the door clear.

Sophie broke the kiss but she made no move to run. She

pushed his coat down his arms with impatience, at the same time her bodice fell in a wash of crumpled silk.

David's heart sped as he let his coat drop to the floor. Beneath the bodice was Sophie's corset, a small one to fit under the breath of a bodice.

He loosened the corset with skilled fingers, pulling out the laces with ease. Under that was her combinations, her breasts unfettered beneath.

Sophie unbuttoned David's waistcoat as he unfastened her skirt. The gown was beautiful—he recognized a masterful touch in its making—but Sophie underneath was even more beautiful.

The warmth of her sparked fire as he shoved the exquisite skirts and petticoats away, lifting Sophie from them when they pooled at her feet. She yanked at the buttons of his shirt, David laughing at her fervor as he closed his arms around her.

She was as soft and pliant as he'd imagined, nothing between them now but her combinations and stockings. David's shirt opened under her urgent fingers, and he couldn't stop a groan as her touch landed on his bare skin.

"My love." He kissed her neck, then traced its curve with his tongue. "Sophie, I have wanted you for so long."

"Highly improper," she murmured.

"I think you know me well enough to realize I don't give a damn."

Her look was impish. "I meant it is highly improper how much I've been wanting *you*. In my uncle's vicarage, no less. I wanted to kiss you and touch you ..."

"Stop." David's need flared high. "You're going to kill me."

"I'd never hurt you." Sophie's voice went soft. "But I think we both needed some relief."

"I love that you are wicked." David tugged her closer. "Never as wicked as me, but I can teach you if you'd like."

Sophie touched his face. "I *would* like that."

"Hell."

All teasing fell away. David swept Sophie into his arms and carried her to the bed. He made short work of her undergarments, Sophie laughing as she helped him.

One thing he liked about a kilt—he could unbelt it and unwind it quickly, no stumbling over clumsy trousers. The swaths of plaid came open, loosening and falling away.

He spread the plaid on the bed, surrounding Sophie with his Scottish ancestry, and slid off the drawers he wore beneath—no traditional bareness for David.

He took a moment to study her—full breasts, waist nipped in a little from corsets, lush hips, lovely legs that had always been hidden by skirts. He'd glimpsed those legs from time to time as they'd scrambled around Dr. Pierson's excavation, brief flashes of calf, and once a very enticing hint of thigh when he'd helped her out of the hole where the mosaic lay. Enough to make him hot and breathless and deprive him of sleep for days.

Now she was here, in his bed. David hadn't used this room in years—it was fitting he re-enter this house and chamber as a new man with Sophie.

He was on the bed beside her in the next moment, her body silken under his touch. His shirt still hung from his arms, but he couldn't be bothered to shrug it off.

"Your uncle ruined my hands," David said, spreading one across her belly. In spite of his gloves, his skin had become rough, palms hardened from the work. "Making me dig like a garden laborer."

Sophie caught his hand and kissed it. "I think it's perfect."

"The kindness of you." David brushed her lips with his fingertips.

"You make me want to be kind."

"Hmm, I am not certain that's a compliment. You make *me* want to be very, very bad."

Her smile undid him. "I think I shouldn't mind."

Sophie's answer, coupled with the heat in her eyes, sent David's thoughts to wicked places. He cupped her breast, loving its weight against his palm, then ran his hand down to the join of her legs.

She was ready for him, liquid heat. David slid over her, kissing her as he positioned himself.

She welcomed him in. David closed his eyes, becoming complete for the first time in his life as he slid inside her. Sophie surrounded him, held him, and David knew the fire of pleasure and love.

Sophie wanted to cry out as David thrust deep inside her. This was new, an awareness, a longing, a *need* she'd never experienced.

This was not her first time with a man, yet she felt raw, eager, passionate. David slid into her, hard, but there was no hurting— her body wanted him. This was her David, the man as gentle as he was sinful. He touched her, kissed her, and smiled at her, before he closed his eyes and groaned.

Sophie's answering groan mingled with his. He took such care of her, though he didn't hold back, his thrusts powerful. She knew she was truly *with* him as he loved her, and was in a place he wanted to be. David brushed her hair back with a hard hand, kissed her lips, stroked her skin, looked into her eyes without worry.

"My beautiful lady." His words were filled with quiet desire.

"If I'd known how this would feel, I never could have stayed away from you."

Sophie wanted to answer with witty words, to tell him what he meant to her. She could only touch him, whisper his name.

David didn't seem to mind. He sped his thrusts, each one fire. Sophie clutched at him, the shirt that enticingly bared his shoulders coming off in her frenzy. The folds landed on the plaid, the fine lawn and wool cradling them both.

David's skin was smooth over hard muscle. She felt his heart swiftly beating, his breath on her skin, his kisses. Most of all she felt *him* inside her, opening her, spreading her, remaking her.

Wildness swept her body, and she heard her voice ringing through the firelight. Wordless cries sprang from her throat, a dark, hot ferocity closing her in a crushing grip.

David awakened her, freed her. She met him thrust for thrust, his voice rumbling as he groaned her name, the sound like velvet.

I love you! Sophie shouted silently. She might have said it out loud—she wasn't certain.

The wildness took her far away on a whirlwind of sensation, then receded, very, very slowly.

After a long time, the world stopped spinning, and she realized she lay on a soft bed, safe in David's arms. He kissed her lips, her face, nipping, whispering, loving.

"My Sophie." He licked the shell of her ear. "My love. My lady."

Sophie could only cup his face, kiss his mouth, and love him.

SOPHIE WOKE TO DAWN LIGHT. IT TRICKLED THROUGH THE window to halo David next to her in a tangle of sheets and plaid.

He must have covered them in the night while Sophie lay insensible from the third time he'd taken her.

Laurie had never brought her to life as David had, never lifted her to the place of unrestrained frenzy. She blushed to think of the things she'd said and done with David in the night.

His cock rested heavily against her thigh, hard with arousal. He must be having a nice dream.

As though he felt her gaze, David opened his eyes. He smiled, relief on his face. "Love. There you are."

"I'd hardly run through the house in my altogether." Sophie skimmed her fingers along his arm, enjoying the strength of him. "And anyway, I was asleep."

David regarded her quietly with his gray-blue eyes. "I feared this would prove to be a dream."

"On the contrary, I think your dreams were quite randy." Sophie let her hand drift to his hardness, and David's smile turned sinful.

"Oh, they were. Would you like me to tell you about them?"

"Will you think me very wicked if I say yes?"

"I will think you wonderful."

"Then yes." Sophie squeezed, and David let out a groan.

"I believe I will show you instead." David growled as he rolled her down into the bed, parting her legs and sliding into her once more.

Sophie laughed and happily succumbed.

When she woke the next time, more hours had passed, and David was gone.

Sophie sat up quickly. She flushed with embarrassment when she saw that a dressing gown had been left for her, along with one of her own shirtwaists and skirt, stockings and sensible shoes, easy things to put on herself. Eleanor must have brought them.

The plaid still lay across the bed, and Sophie spent a moment hugging it to herself, reveling in the sensation of the wool on her skin, the warmth it held of David.

Once she persuaded herself to leave the bed, she dressed hastily, hoping David would return and offer to button her, escort her downstairs, or even simply say good morning. He never appeared.

Sophie's hair was a mess, but she managed to untangle it with a hairbrush that had magically appeared, and pull it into a simple plait. Eleanor had thoughtfully supplied a ribbon and some pins so Sophie could at least wind the braid into a knot and secure it in place.

She wondered if Eleanor sometimes had to dress herself quickly after a night of debauchery, and so knew exactly what Sophie would need. The way the duke and duchess regarded each other when they thought no one watched told her this was the case.

Eleanor sent Sophie a broad smile when she entered the breakfast room. Hart was there, engrossed in a newspaper. His two sons ate with robust appetites and only a modicum of arguing —they were far too busy shoveling in food for brotherly conversation.

Hart gave Sophie a welcoming nod, as he did every morning, then returned to his paper. The boys shouted their greetings, and young Alec rose to hold a chair for her.

Ian and Beth Mackenzie had spent the night, and were at the breakfast table, Ian reading alongside Hart. Beth's greeting shared Eleanor's knowing smile, to Sophie's discomfiture. Ian continued reading without glancing up, but Sophie knew he was in no way trying to be rude.

Of David, there was no sign.

"Mr. Fleming raced away to Shropshire this morning," Eleanor said, placidly buttering her bread. "Your uncle sent him a telegram."

"Oh." Sophie accepted the coffee a footman poured her, and young Malcolm brought her toast. "Thank you," she said to them both.

"Dr. Pierson sent you a telegram as well." Eleanor pulled a small envelope from her pocket. "Well, it was the same telegram, as your uncle no doubt wanted to save the expense of sending two identical ones. He seems to believe he'd find the two of you in one place."

Sophie's face went hot, and Eleanor's eyes glinted with good humor as she handed over the paper.

Sophie opened it and scanned its contents. Uncle Lucas had indeed been economical: *Amazing developments. You must come. L.P.*

Her agitation grew—Uncle did not dispense telegraph messages without cause. "I must go, then," she said, half rising.

"After breakfast," Eleanor advised. "David has already gone to calm him. There's a train at ten."

"David—I mean, Mr. Fleming—could not wait until ten?" Sophie resumed her seat and carefully spread butter across her toast, moving the knife to all corners.

"Hadn't you better call him David now?" Eleanor asked with her unnerving candor. "He decided to go ahead of you, and I agreed with him. Do not be alarmed. All will be well."

Beth, next to Eleanor, nodded agreement.

Hart was obviously listening to the conversation—his eyes had become fixed on the page—and now he lowered the newspaper and pinned Sophie with his golden gaze. "David is my closest friend. He needs happiness, no matter how much he pretends to deny it." His expression softened. "I am grateful to you for giving it to him."

Sophie set down her toast, untasted. "I've done nothing."

"Don't rush them, Hart." Eleanor put her elbows on the table and raised a cup to her lips. "And you call *me* an impatient matchmaker."

"Because you are." Hart sent her a look that heated the air. "A confounded interfering busybody."

Eleanor put out her tongue at him. "But a successful one."

Hart gave her another scorching glance, then a pointed one at Sophie before returning to his newspaper. The lads were quiet, watching the adults with interest.

Ian laid down his paper with a quiet rustle and met Sophie's gaze without a flicker.

"You are good for him," he said. "There is also a train at half past eight."

Ian studied her for a moment longer, then gave a nod, as though he'd finished, and went back to his paper.

Beth watched her husband with love in her eyes. "I can help you pack your things," she offered to Sophie.

Sophie gulped coffee and clattered the cup to its saucer. She had no appetite, and her feet urged her to run, run, run, all the way to Shropshire, where David waited.

She rose, her chair banging. "No need for packing. I have things at Uncle's. Thank you, Eleanor, for your kind invitation. Could you have a hansom summoned for me?"

All but Ian looked up at her, every face interested.

"Hart's coach should be at the front door momentarily," Eleanor said. "I'd anticipated you'd want to go at once, and hansoms can be unsavory. You'd best be off, my dear. Do greet your uncle for me."

CHAPTER 18

*D*avid wandered the abbey ruins, one eye on the path to the vicarage below. The field with the Roman villa lay in the distance, tiny figures moving about the earth there.

He had to admit that Dr. Gaspar had done remarkable work. He and Pierson had uncovered more of the mosaic and then discovered a wall with an intact painting—a trompe l'oiel of a window into a garden.

This had been the "amazing development" that had made Dr. Pierson send an excited message summoning David and Sophie, the two of them at the same time. As though they belonged together.

David had departed at once, for reasons of his own, leaving Sophie to sleep.

Now he wondered if she'd bother coming. Why should she desert Eleanor's very comfortable house for the mist and rain of Pierson's fields? She could view Pierson's discoveries at any time. David would end up climbing back onto a train, chugging to London, and having his tete-a-tete with her in the Grosvenor Square house with the very nosy Mackenzies looking on.

At least Griffin wasn't at the dig. As David suspected, the overly pampered man would stay home until Pierson and Dr. Gaspar unearthed the entire villa and then swan in and claim the credit. Ah well. Griffin's funding would let Pierson excavate to his heart's content and provide a salary to the penniless Gaspar. Best of all, Griff would leave David alone. All thanks to Sophie.

Dr. Pierson appeared far below along the path to the villa, walking briskly. After a moment, a woman rushed to catch up to him with a flurry of skirts, a large hat shielding her from the mists. She fell into step with Pierson—he was taking her to see the mural.

David stilled, his blood flashing cold, then hot.

True, a wall painting from ancient times was rare and important. But to David, at this moment, it didn't matter at all.

He leaned on a ruined stone wall and watched them. He could rush down and across the mile of field and join them, but David feared if he did so, the spell that had woven around him and Sophie would break.

She'd evaporate, never having existed, or worse, she'd look at him with neutral welcome and be far more interested in seeing her uncle's wall than David. Or she'd be ashamed of how beautiful and uninhibited she'd been in his bed.

The memory flared of her rising to his touch, her hot kisses on his flesh—and David's body responded. Most inconvenient while he stood on a cold hilltop, the bones of an ancient scriptorium for company.

Sophie's steps were animated on the path below, her excitement about Pierson's find evident. They disappeared behind trees for a long moment, then emerged even farther away, Gaspar coming to greet them.

David burned as Gaspar took Sophie's hand. He balled his hands on the stone wall, ready to dash down and rip Gaspar away from her, but he stopped himself. He'd look like a fool, and Sophie would disdain him.

She was here. That was all that mattered.

Sophie spoke with the archaeologists for a long time, vanishing toward the villa with Pierson and emerging ten minutes later. Dr. Gaspar hovered next to her, but Sophie turned from him and embraced her uncle. Congratulating Pierson, happy for him.

They stepped apart, Sophie tilting her head to look up at Pierson, her body conveying inquiry. Dr. Pierson glanced about as though searching for something, then he turned and pointed at the abbey on the hill.

David froze. Sophie couldn't possibly see him hiding up here, but he felt her gaze as she peered at the ruins.

She settled her hat, waved at the gentlemen, and began her ascent toward the abbey.

David's body went ice cold. Dratted wind.

He rushed about, kicking aside pebbles and dusting off the top of the wall on which he'd leaned, as though tidying his house for a visitor. Ridiculous. He made himself cease and leaned on a stone pillar, as though he'd come here to do nothing more than a little birdwatching.

Even so, his heart raced as she walked up the hill, taking her time. It was a steep climb, after all, but David could wait no longer.

He gave up his pose and jogged down to meet her, escorting her the last yards. When they reached level ground at the top of the hill, Sophie did not remove her hand from the crook of his arm, her gloved fingers warm.

"The wall they've found is lovely," she said with enthusiasm. "Colors quite beautiful."

"Indeed worthy of the command that dragged me from

London at an ungodly hour," David said, pleased he could speak with his usual sarcasm. "Oh, forgot. No hour is ungodly. Just dark, cold, and disagreeable."

Sophie smiled at his feeble wit. "You did not have to rush off, you know. We could have traveled together."

"I wanted to ask your uncle a few questions. And if I'd been alone with you in a train carriage ..." David glanced down and found her green eyes on him—the eyes that had filled with passion last night in the firelight.

He thought of the many things they could have done in a train carriage, in spite of the cramped space. It involved Sophie's legs around him as she faced him on his lap, or she on her knees on the seat ...

David gulped a lungful of cold wind and forced the images away. He'd never be able to speak, let alone stand up, if he continued with his fantasies.

"What did you wish to ask Uncle Lucas about?" Sophie's look was innocent—she couldn't read his mind, thank heaven.

"Oh ... one or two things. One was whether he'd decided to stay in Shropshire and bury himself in his Roman villa or rush to foreign parts."

"What did he answer?"

David shrugged, pretending nonchalance. "He says he is not certain. The villa is proving more complex than he realized. So he is remaining here for now. Which suits me."

"Are you going to stay and help him?"

Her question was so hopeful that David wanted to kiss her. "Possibly. It would do me good, rusticating in the country and letting Town life go hang. Though I do want to make improvements to my own house—I can be a social recluse there instead. And ... well, Gaspar rubs me the wrong way. I'm not sure how long I can stick him."

"He's a bit shy, is all." Sophie flashed a sudden smile. "He asked me to marry him."

David went still, his heart beating thickly as pain shot through his body. Gaspar was exactly the sort of man Sophie should marry—respectable, learned, unworldly. She would rush to him, leaving David in her dust.

He drew a hoarse breath. "Did he?"

She nodded, serene. "He knew about my predicament with Laurie, and he offered to save me from ruin. I turned him down, of course. But it was kind of him."

"Kind?" David's lips were so stiff, the word barely formed, but the rest of his body flooded with relief. She'd said no. "It wasn't kindness, my dear. He wanted you." He gazed down at the path to the ruins, a growl in his throat. "Probably still does."

Sophie looked perplexed. "Dr. Gaspar? He never said such a thing. Nor would he."

"Any man looking at you wants you. In his bed." David scowled. "Trust me."

How could they not? With her wide smile that made him hot all over, those beautiful green eyes that assessed him with intelligence she didn't bother to hide—how could any man resist her?

"I very much doubt that," she said with a faint laugh.

"I assure you, my dear, it is true."

Sophie slanted David a glance that immediately made him hard. "You mean that whenever I walk into a gathering—a soiree perhaps, or a discussion on the latest improving novel—every gentleman there looks at me and thinks of bed? That is absolute nonsense, unless his thoughts are only on sleep."

David didn't laugh. "I know what goes on in the heads of the male sex, and they would think this." He reached to touch her cheek. "How could they help it?"

Sophie dimpled under his fingertips. "All of them? Even Mr. Gladstone?"

David drew a breath to answer, then dropped his hand. "Perhaps not. He is a bit prim. Or, he *would* think it, but never let on."

Amusement sparkled in her eyes. "You are absurd, as is this conversation."

"No, I am a man in love." David let the naked truth come. "When I think of life without you, Sophie, I feel ... empty."

Sophie's laughter vanished, pain behind her eyes. "But you have so much," she said softly. "So many who love you—Uncle Lucas, Eleanor, Hart and his family. Dear friends who will do anything for you."

"I know. Ungrateful wretch that I am." David removed his hat and dropped it to the ground, not caring that it rolled immediately to a corner of the wall and into a puddle. "But without *you*, Sophie ..." He shook his head, wind ruffling his hair. "My life was different before I knew you. I didn't realize it was empty, even when vast caverns opened before me. I filled the holes with debauchery and bad people and pretended all was well." He gazed at her limply. "But now I know you are in the world, it has become a better place. At least the parts with you in them."

Sophie's voice went soft. "You always flatter me."

"No, I don't." David touched her cheek, drawing fire from her smooth skin. "It isn't flattery, Sophie. I want you to stay with me forever, but I have no business wanting that. I'm a wreck of a man, and you were already bound to an evil idiot." He made himself lift his touch away, to not clutch at her, fall on his knees, and beg her to stay. He'd weep and grovel—anything if she would never go. "I found a way to annul your marriage so you'd be free. And you are. As you were meant to be."

"I am free because of you," Sophie gazed at him with too much gratitude. "I can return to my family and live my life without shame, because of you. Or follow Uncle through the wilderness digging up bits of it if I like."

David gave her a half laugh. "When Pierson drags you out of bed at four in the morning to sift earth under the broiling sun, I imagine you'll curse me."

"Or the mud of England. You said he has not yet fixed on the Near East."

"Don't give me hope." David glanced away from her, resting his gaze on the stones that had sheltered men of God so long ago, when they thought their enclosed world would last forever. "Or maybe I do want hope. Saying good-bye to you ... It is nothing I can do, so I won't."

"David ..."

"And don't say you'll stay with me out of pity. I couldn't bear —" He broke off, swallowing. "No, I am a liar. I could bear your pity without much struggle at all. Because you'd be with me."

Sophie gave him a bleak look that seared his heart. "I never meant to hurt you."

"I don't imagine you did. You don't have it in you."

David glanced away again, drawing strength from the soaring ruins, then turned swiftly to her and seized her hand.

"My dear, I will tell you directly instead of dancing around it: I want you. In my life, by my side, in all ways. I'm what you always call me—a blackguard—for wanting it. Lackwit Laurie made your life hell. Why should you bind yourself to another man after that?" David forced his self-deprecating smile. "But if you do not want to entangle yourself legally, which I can understand, we could always live in delicious sin. Do as we please, go where we please. You'd always be free to leave me at any time, no questions, no recriminations."

Sophie gazed at him in astonishment. "Could you hold yourself to that—no questions or recriminations?"

"Oh, yes." David nodded fervently. Sophie could do whatever she liked with him, whether wife or mistress. "Though *you* might have a good many of both."

A smile pulled at her lips. "You'd ruin me in truth."

"Not ruined. Celebrated. We wouldn't live among stuffy Englishmen who condemn anything enjoyable while guiltily committing the same sins in secret. We'd travel the world, be welcomed by princes and kings—they have terrible manners but excellent wine."

Sophie laughed, her green eyes so beautiful. "You are ridiculous."

"I am. I can't help myself. I always will be." David drew another breath. "But I want to be ridiculous with you at my side. As my mistress, as my wife—which one will make no difference to *me*." He caught her other hand and pulled her closer. "I want to share my life with you, Sophie Tierney. On whatever terms you wish."

Sophie flushed, her uncertainty breaking his heart. "The carefree bachelor will throw away *his* freedom?"

"It isn't freedom, dear lady. It is loneliness. I watched the young Hart Mackenzie pretend to be wild and free—his original plan for life was to marry a woman, set her up in a house, and leave her there while he did what he pleased. Then he met Eleanor, and she changed everything. I learned from Hart and El what it means to share a life, and that is what I want. To share my life, as wretched as it is, with you."

Sophie's lips had parted, and now they trembled, but she remained silent. Trying to decide how to turn him down gently? It couldn't be done.

David's words became edged with despair. "I'll understand if you'd prefer to run far way, to dig up the world with Pierson and forget about the hell your life has been. I will not blame you." He made himself release her hands, to take a step back from her, to let her go. "I will only miss you. And love you."

When Sophie said nothing, David's pain gripped him. He pressed his hands together to try to summon the serenity of this place, but it eluded him. Perhaps he could be like the monks, withdrawing from the world to do nothing but tend his garden and carefully inscribe words in books.

Sophie was so beautiful in the sunlight, the green of her hat's ribbon bringing out her eyes. He wanted to look upon her every day, drink her in, to let her save his life by simply being in her presence.

But he wouldn't trap her. Her ass of a husband had done so, and David would never crush her like that.

"I'll go," he forced himself to say. "Don't worry, my love. I won't follow you about like a lovesick swain writing you terrible poetry or showering you with bouquets of meaningful flowers. My friends would sit on my head and stop me even if I tried."

A sob escaped Sophie's throat. She stepped to him and caught the lapels of his coat.

"Idiot." Her voice was choked. "I don't want you to go, or to send me terrible poetry or bushels of flowers. I want *you*. I love *you*, my dear, dear David."

And she kissed him.

David started as Sophie's lips warmed him and her tears dropped, burning, to his skin. In the next instant, he dragged her into his arms, a flood of release washing his heart.

He kissed her as amazement and hope, love and happiness poured through him and made him want to weep.

David broke the kiss and took her face between his hands—her lovely, lovely face whose mouth had just spoken those beautiful words.

"Love?" he demanded. "Actual love? Damnation, Sophie, don't tease me. Not about this."

Her eyes held honesty. "I wouldn't, I promise. I love you, David. I want to share my life with *you*. Whether we follow Uncle or live in your house in Hertfordshire or dwell in a hovel in the wilderness, makes no difference. I don't want to lose you. In all this madness, you were the one thing I could turn to, the one person who kept me steady."

More astonishment. David held on to her as though saving himself from drowning. "Truly? I must tell my friends. I've never been the steady one."

"Yes, you have." Sophie laughed, her body quivering delightfully. "You've always been there for everyone. It sometimes angers me that your friends don't appreciate you more. You play the cynical, world-weary gentleman, but behind it, you truly care for people. For Hart and Eleanor—you are glad for them, genuinely so. You are terribly fond of Uncle Lucas, or you'd never have sought his company and helped find his villa. You, my friend, are a compassionate and giving man, whether you like it or not."

David gave her a look of mock dismay, but he knew she spoke the truth. He'd been happy to help El and Hart find each other, glad to indulge Pierson, and more than pleased to disentangle Sophie from her bad marriage. He'd always striven to be useful to those he loved.

"A sentimental fool, you mean. Hell, and I thought I concealed that so well."

"Silly man. You have a large heart, which you choose to hide for some daft reason. But I see it." Sophie touched his chest, and her voice went quiet. "I love you for it."

David slid his arms around her. "I hope you love more than just my heart. Or is that too much to ask?"

Sophie's teasing look, with a touch of wickedness, shot fire through him. "I do think there are other parts of you that I would also like to live with."

"Oh?" David's heart hammered. "Do tell."

"I'd rather show you instead."

David touched his forehead against hers. "Wicked lass." He kissed her, leisurely but tasting her fire. "*Beautiful* lass. Do you know how beautiful?" He brushed his lips over her cheek then behind her ear, following with a nibble of her delectable earlobe. "I love you so. Every inch of you. I believe I will kiss them all now."

"We are standing on a hill."

"Yes, well." David's mouth moved to her temple, the bridge of her nose. "We will have to remedy that."

"With my uncle's vicarage as our only retreat."

David started to laugh. "God bless your uncle. *He* is why I flew here so early this morning. I came to ask for his blessing. I confessed all—my love for you and the fact that I wanted to marry you, more than anything else in this life."

Sophie gave him a puzzled but happy look. "Shouldn't it be my father you ask for my hand?"

"I've never met your father. Besides, your uncle has been like a father to me—my own was too busy being decadent and frivolous to raise a son. Do you know what Pierson said when I asked him?"

Sophie sent him a beautiful smile. "Pray, tell me."

"He blinked and said, 'Of course you love Sophie. Do you mean you haven't asked her yet? Do get on with it, my boy.' And he marched off to his villa."

Sophie burst out laughing. "He is the dearest man in the world."

"He is, but never tell him I said so." David closed his arms around her, Sophie's warmth cutting the cool wind. "Is this your answer, Sophie? You will marry me?"

"Yes." Sophie looked straight at him, and he saw her heart in her eyes—her loving, true, honest heart. "I will marry you, Mr. Fleming."

"Thank God for that," David breathed out, and he kissed her.

And kissed her. The spring wind tried to push them from the hill, but the old ruined wall, which had stood for centuries through strife and English weather, held them steady. David pulled Sophie against him, the curve of her body fitting his, her firm hands on his back keeping him from falling.

He tasted her goodness, her fire, her laughter. He loved this woman with all his strength, and she'd just said she loved him back. The world was an incredible place.

From far away came an excited cry in Pierson's unmistakable shout. *"Eureka!"*

David and Sophie broke apart, eyes wide, then they dissolved into laughter.

They caught each other's hands and ran down the hill toward the vicar who was dancing up and down in the joy of another find.

Their laughter drifted back to the old abbey, the wind carrying it to sigh around its benevolent stones.

EPILOGUE

*S*ophie's ceremony for her second wedding was worlds away from her first.

Absent was the tension, the fear as she was dressed by her attendants—worry she'd be too awkward under the stares of the highest in society, and most especially, Laurie's rigid aunts, sneering uncles, and derisive cousins. Fear she'd trip on her gown, stammer as she repeated the vows, or do something else that disgraced her in the eyes of the aristocrats who'd come to watch the Earl of Devonport take a bride.

Today, she was surrounded by laughter and light. She and David had decided together to marry at his home in Hertford-shire, Moreland Park's garden in June bursting with flowers. They'd collaborated on the guest lists, inviting only their close family and dearest friends. For Sophie's first wedding, Laurie and his aunt had dictated that it would be held in St. George's, Hanover Square, and decided upon the guests without consulting her.

Sophie's ladies for her second wedding were her oldest girl-hood friends as well as the Mackenzie wives. Eleanor chattered away while she took photographs, and Isabella had lent her expertise in designing the gown, which hung from Sophie in elegant swaths of ivory silk.

Beth and Violet helped with the flowers—pink roses in a cascading bouquet for Sophie, buds and baby's breath for the ladies—and Ainsley had been in charge of the cake.

The Mackenzie children played their parts—Lord Alec, the duke's heir, proud in his role of ring bearer. If his brother, Mal, let him appear without being muddy, bloody, and his suit torn, all would be well. The younger Mackenzie girls would scatter flower petals for Sophie while the older girls and the lads made sure the guests were looked after.

"You are beautiful," Eleanor declared as she clicked her camera, this a small affair that held the newfangled celluloid film. "David will swoon when he sees you. I cannot wait."

The ladies laughed hard at the idea of the suave David doing anything so inelegant as swooning, but Sophie barely smiled. She longed to be near him, to take his hand and be his wife, and she chafed for the ceremony to begin.

Isabella peered at her knowingly. "No wilting bride here. I believe she'll be glad when we clear off and let her be alone with the dashing Mr. Fleming."

Sophie's face heated, and the ladies went off in another peal of laughter.

During the wedding preparations, she and David had vowed they'd wait to touch each other again until after the marriage ceremony. They'd begin their wedding trip tomorrow with a visit to Uncle Lucas in Shropshire, and then a sojourn to the Continent to look at ruins in Rome and Pompei. They'd also planned plenty of time in lavish hotels along the way, where they could explore each other to their heart's content as man and wife. No reason to rush.

That lofty sentiment had lasted until Sophie encountered David in the corridor late last night, she returning from seeing that her guests were comfortable.

They'd met in the shadows, and David had blown out the candle Sophie had carried. His bedchamber had been nearby, and after a time of hot kisses in the corridor, she'd willingly let him lead her inside.

Fortescue had betrayed no surprise when he entered in the morning to find Sophie curled up against David, only inquired what she'd like to have brought for breakfast. David had snarled at him, but then ordered a large breakfast for himself, as long as Forty was offering.

Tonight, Sophie would share David's bed as his wife.

When she'd realized at her first wedding that her husband's bed awaited, she'd trembled and felt sick. Today, she longed to race through the proceedings so she could take David into her arms and lose herself in him.

I love him. That was the difference, she realized. She loved David deeply, with all her being. When he'd suggested living in sin instead of the respectability of marriage, Sophie had been ready to agree in a heartbeat.

This wedding ceremony would allow the solicitors and the church to mark the union down as legal and acceptable. The love and togetherness after that was for David and Sophie alone.

When Isabella's daughter Aimee announced it was time, Sophie nearly ran from the room. The Mackenzie ladies followed her with much merriment.

As the weather held fair, they'd marry in the garden. Sophie walked out to sunshine, a cool breeze, and a riot of roses, geraniums, snapdragons, zinnias, and others in myriad colors.

The guests were mostly in their places, though many still milled about, friends talking, joking, laughing—no stiff concern or formality. Elliot McBride chased his son and youngest daughter across the green, both children somehow outrunning his long legs, their screams of mirth cutting the air. His older daughter raced after them, black curls dancing, she laughing as she helped Elliot catch her brother and sister.

Daniel lifted his own daughter when she tried to join the hunt, planting her on his shoulders as he and Violet took their seats.

Sophie saw most of this in a blur, her focus all for the man who waited next to the vicar under the flower-strewn arbor.

Uncle Lucas had persuaded the local vicar to let him perform the actual ceremony. The vicar, happy to put up his feet and sip sherry instead, nodded contentedly in the sunshine in the first row, while Uncle Lucas stood proudly in his vestments, ready to marry Sophie to David.

Hart Mackenzie, his expression a mixture of relief and gladness, stood beside David as his groomsman. Eleanor had told Sophie in private that Hart was very pleased with this marriage. Not only was he happy for his friend, but Hart could cease feeling contrite that he'd found happiness in marriage while David had wandered alone.

"Hart loves David," Eleanor had confided. "Only never tell him I said so. He'd deny it with every breath. David, too. When anyone mentions how close the pair of them are, they both contrive to look surprised."

The two now stood rather stiffly together, it amused Sophie to see. The best of friends, each holding up the other through pain, heartache, and loss. Well, she'd let their love for each other be her and El's secret.

David was the only person in the crowd at the moment who was clear and sharp to Sophie. His smile touched her, that pleased smile with a hint of self-deprecation that meant he was so very happy inside.

Her father, who'd been introduced to the pleasure of Mackenzie malt last night, was a bit red about the eyes this morning, but led Sophie down the aisle for the second time in her life. At Laurie's wedding, her father had been worried, hugging her and reluctant to let her go. This time, he was smiling, having found friends in David, Hart, and the other Mackenzies. When Sophie had peeped into the dining room last evening after the ladies had left it, she'd seen her father deep in conversation with Hart and David, laughing at Mac's drawling interjections, and listening with interest at anything Ian had to add.

Ian Mackenzie stood in the second row. He slanted Sophie a glance as she passed and gave her a nod, as though thanking her. Sophie smiled back at him, and was rewarded with a sudden and pleased grin.

David's expression softened as she stepped next to him. "How beautiful you are," he whispered. He leaned closer. "I want to eat you up."

Sophie blushed hard, and Hart nudged David. "Contain yourself, Fleming. We have a long ceremony to get through."

David sent him an innocent look, and Sophie laughed. Uncle Lucas, not as naive as he sometimes appeared, narrowed his eyes.

"Be seemly, Fleming," Pierson said. "I know fisticuffs, if you recall."

David touched the side of his face. "I remember."

"You were eighteen," Hart rumbled.

"Yes. It was a blow that lasted me ages." David winked at Sophie. "I well deserved it."

"I allowed you to defend yourself," Uncle Lucas said in a pained voice. "You simply didn't pay attention to your lessons.

Now then, *We are gathered together here in the sight of God, to join together this man and this woman ....*"

His voice rose, and the crowd quieted, the children ceased their shrieking and running, friends converging to watch David and Sophie marry.

Sophie studied David as her uncle's soothing voice went on. She recalled how David had lifted his head at the breakfast table the morning she'd met him, his eyes red-rimmed and bleary, his hair a mess, face unshaven. And yet, she'd felt the heat of him, the spark that woke her from her stupor. She'd looked into his eyes and lost a part of herself.

A part he'd never hurt. Sophie understood as he gazed at her now that she too held a part of him. They'd shared themselves, not only bodies but hearts, souls, secrets.

A true marriage, she thought as she squeezed his arm, strength enclosed by soft cashmere. A joining of thoughts and respect, love and wanting.

A forever bond, and one just for them.

David leaned to her again. "I love you."

The whispered words warmed her to her toes. Sophie's heart swelled, the freedom he'd given her to love and trust sweeping aside the last dust of her sorrows.

"I love *you*," she said into his ear, against the rise and fall of Uncle Lucas's voice. "My dearest darling, thank you."

"It was my pleasure." David grinned at her. "How else could I repay the woman who saved my life?"

Sophie broke all precedence for wedding ceremonies by rising on her tiptoes and kissing David on the lips.

The crowd behind them cheered. Applause, laughter, whoops, and shouts made Uncle Lucas look up from his open book. Hart laughed, the rumble deep and vibrating.

David slid his arms around Sophie and let the kiss deepen, never mind the escalating noise around them.

"Bless you," he whispered as they drew apart once more. His fingers were warm as he brushed her hair back from her face. "You are the best woman in the world."

"*I* knew that," Uncle Lucas broke in. "Took you long enough to realize, Fleming." He loudly cleared his throat and raised his voice. "Wilt though have this woman to be thy wedded wife?"

David's shout—"I will!"—rang through the summer air, mingling with the laughter.

Sophie took his hands and said, "I will," just as readily, something loosening in her heart as she joined with him in true and lasting love.

AUTHOR'S NOTE

*T*hank you for reading!

The Mackenzie clan returns in *A Mackenzie Yuletide*. Ian determines to find Beth the best Christmas gift of all time, with help from his daughters and son. Return to Scotland for another Mackenzie adventure!

(*A Mackenzie Yuletide* is available as a standalone e-book, or in e-book and print in the anthology *A Mackenzie Clan Christmas*.) Please turn the page for an excerpt!

EXCERPT: A MACKENZIE YULETIDE

December 1898

$\mathcal{M}$ ac Mackenzie paused, his paintbrush dripping, at the soft sound from the end of the corridor.

The skylights in his room at the top of Kilmorgan Castle, the vast Mackenzie manor house, were dark. Mac didn't remember night falling, but when he became deeply immersed in painting, time passed swiftly.

It was also cold, his fire having died to a glow of coals. Lamps glowed softly, which meant his valet, Bellamy, must have entered and lit them.

Mac pulled himself out of the painting of a Scottish landscape and restored himself to the here and now. It was mid-December, at two in the morning, and his wife and children were snugly asleep in the floors below. Mac's brothers and their families slept in their wings of the vast house, all awaiting the celebrations at Christmas and Hogmanay.

No one should be up near the studio at this hour, but that did not mean his son, Robert, hadn't climbed restlessly out of bed to roam the halls. Or that Robert and his cousins Jamie and Alec hadn't gathered for a stolen smoke or nip of whisky they didn't think their fathers knew about.

Mac wiped his brush and dropped it into his jar of oil of turpentine. He mopped at his hands, which never stayed clean, but didn't bother trying to scrub off his face. Nor did he remove the kerchief that kept his hair more or less free of paint. Once he found the source of the noise, he'd return and finish the shadowing that was challenging him.

He shrugged on his shirt, now noticing the cold. Painting with fervor heated his body, so he usually ended up in only his kilt and shoes.

Mac stepped into the cold, silent hall. It ran narrowly before him, ending in a T—one direction led to Ian's wing, the other to Cameron's. He saw a flutter of white in the shadows, heard again the quiet rustle that had cut through his painting haze.

"Iz?" Mac called softly.

He started down the corridor. If Isabella, his darling wife, had come up to entice him to bed, he'd play along. The studio had a wide, comfortable sofa, and he could build up the fire to keep them warm while they bared more skin . . .

Another flutter, then silence.

Mac began to grin. Isabella had a teasing streak, and when she turned playful, life became splendid. Mac's blood warmed, and he forgot all about painting.

"Izzy, love." He started after her, anticipation building. What game would she play this time? And how would Mac turn the tables, as he loved to do?

He reached the split in the corridor. Stairs led down from here to the floors below, or he could turn to one of his brothers' wings. Years ago, the sons and daughters of the Mackenzies had slept in nurseries on these top floors, but they had long since moved to larger bedchambers below.

That fact was in one way sad, but then again, the older children would be marrying in a few short years, and nurseries would fill again. Mac's adopted daughter, Aimee, was nineteen now, and so beautiful.

Which was very worrying. Mac found himself snarling like a bear at gentlemen she danced with at the balls Isabella had carefully selected since Aimee's debut.

An icy draft poured over him as he tried to decide which way to turn. The wind cut, making him shiver. Who had left a blasted window open?

He thought the chill came from Cam's wing, and he quietly moved that direction. The short hall beyond was empty and dark.

"What the devil are you doing, love?" he said, a bit louder. "It's freezing. Let's go to the studio and make it cozy."

Another rustle. Mac followed the noise around the corner to the longer corridor. At its end was a flash of white, then nothing.

Mac gave up stealth and sprinted down the corridor. He'd catch Isabella and she'd laugh, then he'd carry her to where they could tear off what little clothing Mac wore and enjoy themselves.

A window lay at the end of the hall—open, Mac saw as he reached it. As he'd suspected. Mac slammed it closed.

He heard a whisper of sound and spun around. Behind him, where he'd just come from, stood a lady in white. A chance moonbeam caught on her red hair.

In that instant, Mac knew this wasn't Isabella. Different stance, different height, and Isabella was . . . alive.

Why he thought this woman wasn't, Mac didn't know. Maybe because the moonlight made her skin deathly pale, or because the white dress floated, though the draft had gone. Mac couldn't see every detail of her, but she seemed to have no hands or feet.

Mac's heart beat faster, but he felt no fear. Kilmorgan was an old place—this could be any lady, from any era.

"Good evening," he said softly. "I'm Mac. But you probably know that. What's *your* name, lass? Which one are you?"

The apparition was utterly silent. Mac took a step forward, wondering what would happen when he reached her. Could he walk straight through her? And would that be impolite?

He was halfway down the hall to the hovering lady when she vanished, abruptly and utterly.

Clouds slid over the moon. Mac was left in the freezing cold and dark, alone, disappointed, and suddenly tired.

He moved quickly back to his own wing, doused the lights in the studio, and fled downstairs to his bedchamber, which was warm and inviting. His wife was fast asleep in their bed, and never moved when Mac climbed in with her, spooning close to her in their heated nest.

———

"I saw a ghost last night," Mac announced at the breakfast table.

Ian Mackenzie took a moment to decide whether this declaration was interesting enough for him to look up from the letter and photographs that had arrived in the morning's post. Mac liked to spin yarns, and Ian had learned to ignore most of them.

He glanced at Mac, who slid into a place at the long table, his plate loaded with eggs, sausages, ham, and scones dripping with butter. A few rivulets of butter trickled over the edge of the plate to make perfect round pools on the tablecloth.

Their nephew Daniel laughed. "Did you, Uncle Mac?"

"I did," Mac answered without worry. "Vanished before my eyes."

Violet, Daniel's wife, made sure their seven-year-old daughter, Fleur, wasn't giving too many bits of toast to the dogs, and leaned forward eagerly. "Interesting. Where did you see it?"

"My wing. Then it floated to Cam's wing and disappeared." Mac shoved most of a scone into his mouth and chewed noisily.

Ian had difficulty knowing when Mac was teasing or serious. Hart and Cameron were straightforward with their speeches—sometimes loudly so—but Mac made up stories or played with words, bursting out laughing in the middle of them. Ian had learned to wait until Mac wound down to judge whether what he spoke was truth or exaggeration. He returned to his letter and let the others at the table play it out.

Breakfast at Kilmorgan was an informal meal, with food placed on the sideboard for all to enjoy. Some days the ladies indulged in breakfast in bed, but most mornings they made their way to the dining room to eat with the family. The younger Mackenzies were welcome—no banishment because they had not yet reached a specific age. The four brothers had made that decision years ago.

Ian liked the breakfast gatherings. He read his letters or newspapers while various Mackenzies chattered around him. At the house he shared with Beth and his three children, breakfast could be intimate or rowdy, the five of them crammed around the table.

As soon as Mac ceased speaking and began to eat, Ian's daughters, Belle and Megan, entered and helped themselves at the sideboard.

Megan finished filling her plate first and took a seat next to Ian. Megan was thirteen now, and becoming so beautiful. Ian lost himself in looking at her eyes, so like her mother's, and her hair that was glossy brown with a touch of red.

Belle, her plate heaped almost as much as Mac's, sat on the other side of her sister. Ian noted they kept to the placement that was usual at home—they knew he preferred it if everyone sat in the same seats day after day.

"Good morning, ladies," Daniel boomed at them. "Uncle Mac has seen a ghost at the top of Kilmorgan Castle. What awful specter haunts our midst? A Highlander of old, calling to his clan? Great-great-grandfather Malcolm bellowing for his whisky? A lady waiting for her lover to return from one of our many rebellions?"

"Papa." Fleur shook her head at him. Like Violet, she was a skeptic.

Megan shivered. "I hope it's not the lonely lady."

Belle scoffed. "There are no ghosts. They are seen only by people who are drunk or mad." She caught Mac's grin and flushed. "Not that I mean you are mad, Uncle Mac. Or drunk. But it has been shown that oil of turpentine and the components of paints can make one's brain behave as though it is intoxicated. You might have breathed in too much last night."

Mac winked at her. "An excellent theory. Very scientific. I assure you, dear niece, I keep plenty of air flowing through my studio and avoid a buildup of fumes. I truly did see a ghost. Kilmorgan is quite haunted."

"Poppycock," Belle said, but Megan shivered again. "There has been absolutely no proven existence of ghosts and spirits," Belle went on. "Those who pretend to have gathered evidence are frauds. Oh, I beg your pardon, Cousin Violet."

"No need, sweetheart," Violet answered calmly. "I know all about frauds and hoaxes. Do not worry, Megan. Whatever your uncle Mac saw, it wasn't a ghost."

"If you say so," Mac said before he fell to devouring the rest of his breakfast.

Megan did not return the smile, from which Ian deduced she was not reassured. He reached over and squeezed her hand.

"There are no ghosts," he said firmly. "They do not exist."

"Quite right," Belle said on Megan's far side.

Belle looked for rational and scientific explanations for everything, from a flower pushing through the earth to how far away the stars were, to how rain clouds formed. Her inquisitive and eager mind had worked through most of the books in Ian's library, and she'd quickly absorbed everything her brother's tutors had taught them.

Jamie, Ian's oldest, had gone off to Harrow, leaving his sisters behind, but Ian had insisted they hire another tutor, one who could keep up with Belle's swift mind. She was determined to go to university, to study to be a doctor. Ian saw no reason why she should not—Belle was brilliant and ought to be allowed to do anything she wanted.

Beth tried to explain to Ian and Belle that education for a woman was very difficult, but Belle only furrowed her brow and said she'd do it. Ian knew she would, and he'd certainly use all his might as a Mackenzie to ensure that she found a university that would take her.

Megan was no less intelligent, but in a different way. She was highly imaginative, constructing entire worlds in her mind and acting them out with her dolls or the dogs. Where Belle made her way through scientific journals, Megan read fairy tales and lengthy novels. Megan was also quite musical, able, like Ian, to learn a piece of music by hearing others play it through once. Unlike Ian, though, Megan could play it back with feeling, often ending up sobbing by the close of the piece.

Megan was compassionate; Belle a force to be reckoned with.

Beth expressed surprise that the two got along so well, but Belle was Megan's defender, and Megan's gentleness eased Belle when she grew frustrated and impatient.

"What is this talk of ghosts?" Isabella Mackenzie floated into the room, her red hair drawn up in the latest fashion, which Ian privately thought resembled a giant pincushion. Isabella changed her hair nearly every week.

Mac rose from the table, wiped his mouth, and kissed his wife soundly on the lips. "Saw one. Upstairs last night."

"How exciting." Isabella helped herself to toast and tea from the sideboard, sat down, and raised her cup to her lips. "Tell me all about it."

Mac launched into his tale once more, and Ian returned to his letter. He'd written to a man in London, asking for particulars on what was in the photographs and line drawings—an antique necklace with intricately worked loops of gold and hung with emeralds and lapis lazuli. It was ancient, Roman, and had purportedly been taken from the tomb of a Roman consul's wife. Somehow it had ended up in the treasury of a church in Norwich, and when the parish needed to raise money, they'd decided to sell it, as it was nonecclesiastical and had been hidden away for a rainy day.

They'd sold it to a small museum in London that hadn't really been able to afford it, and the necklace hadn't proved a great attraction, giant fossil bones being more interesting to the museum's patrons. The museum had quietly sold it on to a collector in Paris.

Ian had decided the necklace would look perfect on Beth, and wanted it for her Hogmanay present.

There was a problem, however. The necklace had disappeared after the sale, and no one knew where it was. Ian, with the determination Belle had inherited from him, set out to find it.

The letter, from a London acquaintance who'd photographed the piece when it had lain in the museum, confessed he did not know where the necklace had ended up. The Frenchman who'd purchased it claimed it had never reached his Parisian mansion. Somewhere between London and Paris, the necklace had vanished.

Ian read the words, studied the man's photographs and drawings of the necklace, and made up his mind that nothing would deter him.

"Excellent," Isabella said. "Once we trap it, we'll know whether it is a true ghost or someone playing tricks on poor, sleepless Mac."

Ian looked up. "Trap it?"

"Yes indeed." Isabella's green eyes sparkled as she gave Ian her wide smile. "We're off to catch a ghost."

"Poor thing," Megan said, her mouth turning down.

"It's only someone playing tricks," Belle said. "You'll see. We'll catch them and give them a good talking-to."

"Poor thing," Megan repeated.

Ian squeezed Megan's hand again and slid one of the photographs toward her. "I'm going to find this for your mama," he said. "Will you help me?"

ALSO BY JENNIFER ASHLEY

Historical Romances

The Mackenzies Series

The Madness of Lord Ian Mackenzie

Lady Isabella's Scandalous Marriage

The Many Sins of Lord Cameron

The Duke's Perfect Wife

A Mackenzie Family Christmas: The Perfect Gift

The Seduction of Elliot McBride

The Untamed Mackenzie

The Wicked Deeds of Daniel Mackenzie

Scandal and the Duchess

Rules for a Proper Governess

The Stolen Mackenzie Bride

A Mackenzie Clan Gathering

Alec Mackenzie's Art of Seduction

The Devilish Lord Will

A Rogue Meets a Scandalous Lady

A Mackenzie Yuletide

(in print in A Mackenzie Clan Christmas)

Historical Mysteries

Kat Holloway "Below Stairs" Victorian Mysteries

A Soupçon of Poison

Death Below Stairs

Scandal Above Stairs

Death in Kew Gardens

Captain Lacey Regency Mystery Series

(writing as Ashley Gardner)

The Hanover Square Affair

A Regimental Murder

The Glass House

The Sudbury School Murders

The Necklace Affair

A Body in Berkeley Square

A Covent Garden Mystery

A Death in Norfolk

A Disappearance in Drury Lane

Murder in Grosvenor Square

The Thames River Murders

The Alexandria Affair

A Mystery at Carlton House

Murder in St. Giles

Death at Brighton Pavilion

MACKENZIE FAMILY TREE

Ferdinand Daniel Mackenzie (Old Dan) 1330-1395
First Duke of Kilmorgan
= m. Lady Margaret Duncannon
|
Fourteen generations
|
Daniel William Mackenzie 1685-1746(?)
(9th Duke of Kilmorgan)
= m. Allison MacNab
|
6 sons
Daniel Duncannon Mackenzie (Duncan) (1710-1746)

William Ferdinand Mackenzie (1714-1746?)
=m. **Josette Oswald**
|
Glenna Oswald (stepdaughter)
Duncan Ian Mackenzie (1748-1836)

Abby Anne Mackenzie (1750-1838)

Magnus Ian Mackenzie (1715-1734)
Angus William Mackenzie (1716-1746)

Alec William Ian Mackenzie (1716-1746?)
=m. Genevieve Millar (d. 1746)
|
Jenny (Genevieve Allison Mary) Mackenzie (1746-1837)

=m2. **Lady Celia Fotheringhay**
|
Magnus Edward Mackenzie (1747-1835)
Catherine Mary Mackenzie (1750-1836)

Malcolm Daniel Mackenzie (1720-1802)
(10th Duke of Kilmorgan from 1746)
= m. **Lady Mary Lennox**
|
Angus Roland Mackenzie 1747-1822
(11th Duke of Kilmorgan)
= m. Donnag Fleming
(ancestor of **David Fleming**)
|
William Ian Mackenzie (The Rake) 1780-1850
(12th Duke of Kilmorgan)
= m. Lady Elizabeth Ross
|
Daniel Mackenzie, 13th Duke of Kilmorgan (1824-1874)
(1st Duke of Kilmorgan, English from 1855)
= m. Elspeth Cameron (d. 1864)

|

Hart Mackenzie (b. 1844)
14th Duke of Kilmorgan from 1874
(2nd Duke of Kilmorgan, English)
= m1. Lady Sarah Graham (d. 1876)

|

(Hart Graham Mackenzie, d. 1876)

= m2. **Lady Eleanor Ramsay**

|

Hart Alec Graham Mackenzie (b. 1885)
Malcolm Ian Mackenzie (b. 1887)

Cameron Mackenzie
= m1. Lady Elizabeth Cavendish (d. 1866)

|

Daniel Mackenzie = m. **Violet Devereaux**

|

Cameron Mackenzie **=** m2. **Ainsley Douglas**

|

Gavina Mackenzie (b. 1883)
Stuart Mackenzie (b. 1885)

"Mac" (Roland Ferdinand) Mackenzie
= m. **Lady Isabella Scranton**

|

Aimee Mackenzie (b. 1879, adopted 1881)
Eileen Mackenzie (b. 1882)
Robert Mackenzie (b. 1883)

Ian Mackenzie = m. **Beth Ackerley**

|

Jamie Mackenzie (b. 1882)
Isabella Elizabeth Mackenzie (Belle) (b. 1883)
Megan Mackenzie (b. 1885)

Lloyd Fellows = m. **Lady Louisa Scranton**

|

Elizabeth Fellows (b. 1886)
William Fellows (b. 1888)
Matthew Fellows (b. 1889)

David Fleming = m. **Sophie Tierney**

|

Lucas Fleming (b. 1894)

McBride Family

Patrick McBride = m. Rona McDougal

Sinclair McBride = m. 1 Margaret Davies (d. 1878)

|

Caitriona (b. 1875)
Andrew (b. 1877)

m. 2 **Roberta "Bertie" Frasier**

|

Marcus (b. 1886)
Elena (b. 1888)

Elliot McBride = m. **Juliana St. John**

|

Priti McBride (b. 1881)
Gemma (b. 1885)
Patrick (b. 1886)

Steven McBride (Captain, Army)
= m. **Rose Barclay**
(Dowager Duchess of Southdown)

|

Helen Rona (b. 1887)

Note: Names in **bold** indicate main characters in the Mackenzie series

ABOUT THE AUTHOR

New York Times bestselling and award-winning author Jennifer Ashley has written more than 100 published novels and novellas in romance, urban fantasy, mystery, and historical fiction under the names Jennifer Ashley, Allyson James, and Ashley Gardner. Jennifer's books have been translated into more than a dozen languages and have earned starred reviews in *Publisher's Weekly* and *Booklist*. When she isn't writing, Jennifer enjoys playing music (guitar, piano, flute), reading, hiking, and building doll-house miniatures.

More about Jennifer's books can be found at
http://www.jenniferashley.com

To keep up to date on her new releases, join her newsletter here:
http://eepurl.com/47kLL

CPSIA information can be obtained
at www.ICGtesting.com
Printed in the USA
LVHW030025030120
642401LV00001B/39/P